SHANNON IN SOMBRA

SARAH SPADE

Cover Art by Fran of Merry-Book-Round

Interior Art by Claire Holt of Luminescence Covers

Exclusive illustration by Nicola of Flourishing Fables

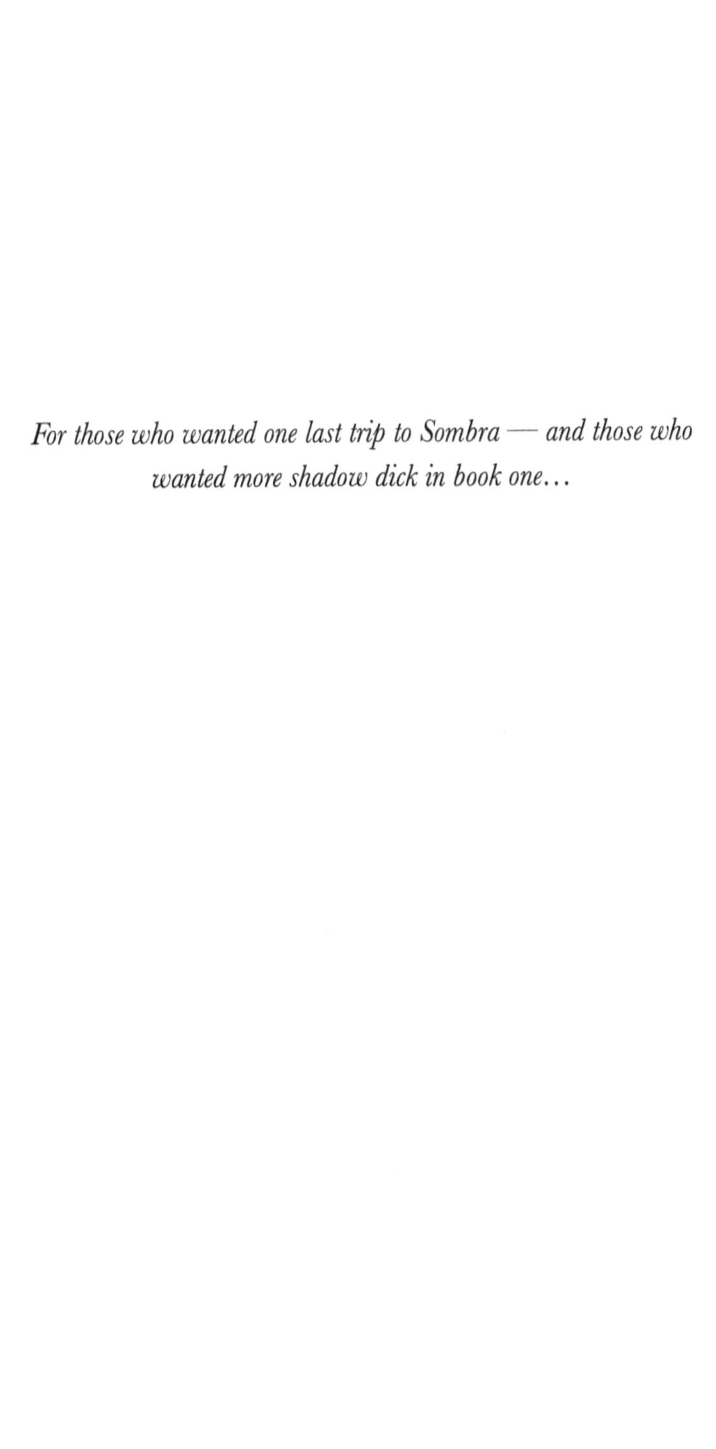

For those who wanted one last trip to Sombra — and those who wanted more shadow dick in book one...

FOREWORD

Thank you for checking out *Shannon in Sombra*!

I always knew that this series would have an over-arching plot, even if—on its surface—they're a bunch of silly, fun monster romances with human women and the devoted demons who love them. By the time Shannon and Amy's stories were told and I started to think about Kennedy, I was halfway to understanding what that would be. The introduction of Hope—plus the first mentions of the mysterious man at the end of the book, and Hope being a fan of Whiskey Rose—really cemented it for me… especially when I decided the final two heroines would be former bandmates of Sierra's.

This book does everything I wanted. It brings Shannon to Sombra, introduces Alana—their daughter who was born at the end of *Taken by the Twins*—and shows some sweet… and some spicy…

moments between Malphas and Shannon before one climax hits—and then another (not as fun) one.

It also answers plenty of questions that have been posed throughout the series! Did you want to know why Haures hid Susanna? Why it's more than a simple coincidence that Sierra, Billie, and Tandy were in their girl group together? Why Freya's bond with Kennedy is more than because she's just a simple pet? And who was that mysterious man who stole the grimoire from Hope and mailed it to Sierra?

Do you want to come along with Shannon to the demon realm and get her opinion on it? On motherhood? Or see a fiercer side to Shannon, plus Malphas's continued love for her even when everything is at stake?

All of that happens in *Shannon in Sombra*, and while this book has light-hearted moments like all the other books in this series—plus open-door spice scenes—it also focuses heavily on their new family dynamic—and what happens when someone tries to jeopardize that. There is a happily-ever-after, though, so even if things get a little tense… there will always be a HEA!

xoxo,
Sarah

PROPHECY

A child born of two worlds,
belonging in both, belonging to none,
will bring with them rain,
and the fires of Sombra will be forever done.

until she summoned a seven-foot-tall demon into her apartment?

A *naked* demon because he was in the bathtub when she reached through worlds and yanked him toward her?

And then she discovered that he was her true love, she was his one true mate, and the two of them would live happily-ever-after—emphasis on *ever* since their mating meant that her immortal shadow demon husband made her immortal, too?

It's true, though. And nearly two years after I gave him my mate's promise, banged the hell out of my demon, and ended up knocked up for my trouble, it's not just the two of us who have gotten the romance-standard HEA.

Four cycles ago—or four months since I might live in Malphas's demon world and speak Sombran now, but good chance I'll always think like a human—I gave birth to our daughter, Alana. And, yes, if you're keeping track, that means I was pregnant for just about a year and a half. I guess I can't complain. Demonesses take three years to gestate. Since our baby gets half her genes from me, half from Mal, I tapped out early, but it was just the right amount of time for Alana.

She is the cutest thing. She has my blonde hair, these tiny black nubs for her demon horns, slightly peachy-colored skin that Mal refers to as colorless instead of, you know, *white*, and a pair of glowing gold eyes that she stole directly from her father. She's well-tempered, advanced for her age, and the best baby ever—and, no, I'm not just biased because I'm her mom. She really is the best.

Oh, and she's also supposedly the child of a prophecy that I've spent the last four months trying to pretend isn't real.

Because of course it isn't just demons and true loves that exist in this world. So do prophecies, and the fantastical idea of a 'chosen one'.

Only, in this case, the chosen one is a half-demon, half-human baby whose birth was supposedly the herald to the end of times in Mal's demon world. Duke Haures, Sombra's ruler for the last two freaking *thousand* years, and the doppelseers, a pair of super freaky twins with the ability to see the future, are convinced that my sweet little baby will either doom Sombra forever or lead it into a new age.

I'm hoping for the latter, personally.

I mean, honestly? How can Alana be Sombra's version of, like, the anti-Christ?

She's not. Point blank. Whatever Lucian and Damien think they saw… whatever Duke Haures believes… she's my sweet, innocent angel, even if I'm looking forward to a couple of hours away from her.

One upside to having a half-demon child? Alana might only be four months old, but she's closer to a human toddler. I feed her from my tit for the sole reason that I produced milk and Sombran formula had a little bit too much ash in it for my taste. Since her first month, though, she's been sleeping through the night and only needs about four feedings a day. Maybe even three if she really sucks it down for lunch.

I feel like she'll be a real kid—and not spawn, because, like how I cling to 'month', I can't go along with referring to my daughter as 'spawn' like the demons do—before she hits her first year. I didn't know what to expect, but I'm not complaining.

Especially since I don't feel that uncomfortable leaving her with a sitter tonight.

I'm not the only human woman who lives in Sombra. These days, there are at least four others who make the demon world their full-time home: Susanna, the duchess of Sombra and Duke Haures's mate; Kennedy, my new best friend, the bookseller who actually sold me the *Grimoire du Sombra* in the first place, and Loki's mate; Billie, Glaine's mate; and Tandy, the most recent addition to our little group, and the lucky chick who got stuck with the doppelseers for the rest of her life.

Apart from Susanna, Kennedy's lived in Sombra longer than any of us. She's also the second human woman to get pregnant by her mate. She's ready to pop any day now which is why, when I mentioned missing having some private time with Malphas, she offered to watch Alana for us.

She thinks of it as practice for when her baby is

here. Me? I'm just happy that someone I trust is willing to take care of Alana for a couple of hours while I reconnect with my mate.

I was cleared to have sex with Mal within the first month after giving birth. Azazel, our village healer, gave me a potion to help me to heal faster. It worked, and I made up for the lost time after my pregnancy got far enough that sleeping with my demon was too awkward with the big belly in the way.

But then, like all new parents, adjusting to having a newborn took its toll. Add that to a complete upheaval of my life as I knew it, and, yeah… sex was put on the back burner for a while.

I had no choice. I always thought that, after Alana was born, the three of us would live together in the human world for a little bit. We even had a nursery all set up for her in the apartment we lived in over the store I took over for Kennedy. My parents are in Florida, our home in Jericho, New York, and I managed to hide my entire pregnancy from them *and* my friends under the guise of being too busy at work.

But then I had Alana. Between the horns and the glowing eyes, I knew I would have to forever hide her. It's one thing keeping my shadow demon mate a secret. Due to Duke Haures's first law, I *had* to or risk the dungeon. But Alana? I couldn't hide my daughter, though I would have to.

And that's when the duke dropped the bomb

It's fucking *awesome*.

Before we left the house—and just so my mate was on the same page as me that by 'walk' I totally meant 'bang'—I stripped down to nothing. Once I realized that I wouldn't be heading back to New York anytime soon, I asked Malphas and Loki to take a quick trip to our place and pack up all of my clothes. I'm not ready to go all native like Kennedy has, wearing woven dresses from the village seamstresses. I'm good with my jeans and tank tops… unless I'm wearing nothing but Mal's shadows.

I love how he can use part of his magic to create his 'coverings'. Not only can he use them to hide my tits, pussy, and ass from the villagers when I'm au natural, but Sombra demons can actually hide their mates in their shadows. So long as he goes from his solid, red-skinned demon form to a hazy mess of shadows with the outline of his horns, arms, legs, and some other appendages on display, he can gather me up in them, and no one knows I'm there.

Well, they probably can guess. Demons in Sombra don't use their shadow form as much as Mal had to in Jericho, so seeing him make his way out of the village in his shadows is probably a honking neon sign that he's about to get laid. Especially when our 'walk' takes him a little out of the way of the village, toward the lava pools on the far side of the ash fields.

Sombra is a dusty, *hot*, fiery world. The farmers grow demon grains, fruits, and vegetables out of the ash with the teensiest, tiniest amount of moisture. In fact, they don't even need rain; based on the prophecy, they'd rather never see the stuff. But that's because the lava pools feed their crops.

Seems like it wouldn't make sense, huh? Lava. Like, actual, literal *lava*. But it does, because in Sombra? The lava—while super hot... because, if I didn't mention it already, Sombra is hot *hot*—has the consistency of water without making you wet.

Even better? As long as Malphas stays in his shadows and keeps me gathered up in them, the sensation of sinking down into the lava pool is almost as relaxing and soothing as easing your tired body into a hot tub. Add in the fact that it can't touch me in Mal's shadows, plus anything he shoots into the pool is disintegrated by the heat immediately, it's no surprise that my kinky side enjoys letting him fuck me in the lava pool.

I'm not the only one, either. Kennedy thinks I'm crazy for it, but I've caught a couple of demon-mated pairs doing the deed in the lava pools, too. I always lead Mal further away for one of our own, but tonight?

Maybe the gods are on my side for once because we're all alone.

Like I said, I have all of my clothes with me in our place. I'd prefer to keep them in one piece as long as I can. That means that undressing and leaving them on the edge of the lava pool is a no-go. I can't risk them somehow getting splashed and ending up incinerated. Or if they accidentally get knocked further into the ash fields and a piece of the volcanic underground incinerates them that way. Nope. It's better to be completely naked and tucked inside of Mal's shadows.

And that doesn't have anything to do with how easy it is to initiate mating with him when he's conveniently bare under his shadows, why would you ask?

I trust Malphas implicitly. If I didn't, I would never willingly walk into a pool of freaking *lava*. He has to keep control of his shadows, but he explained to me once that it was like breathing for a human. He doesn't have to think about how to do it. He just *does* it.

Because Malphas? Like all Sombra demons, he *is* shadow.

Sombra demons don't have just two forms, either. They have *three*. Their solid form, when they turn to inky black shadows, and their mist. What Mal is doing now is keeping his body as his shadows while casting a net with his mist, tucking me inside of it. That's how he can hide me, just like he did the first time I saw Glaine threaten him with the golden chains and a stint in Duke Haures's dungeon.

All I feel is Malphas. All I know is my mate. As he holds my hand, guiding me into the lava pool before jumping in after me, there is a sensation of warm water up against my body without any part of me becoming wet.

Well, no. That's a lie. There's *definitely* a part of me that's wet right now.

Turning into Mal, I grip as much of his sides as I can. I only come up to his sternum when we're standing in front of each other, but that's okay. I'm in the perfect position to scrape my teeth over the first **S** in the tattoo of my name on his chest. As he shudders, I grin, then do it to the **H**. I keep going until the last **N** is a memory, my attention focused on swirling my tongue around his hardened nipple.

When he's in his shadows, that doesn't mean that's all he is. Unless he fades completely to mist or commands his body to turn to pure shadow, there's still a solid body under there somewhere. It's more like his whole form is black, but about two inches of the edge is transparent. I could push my finger through it before finding something hard beneath it.

Right now, my questing fingers find his cock.

The first time we mated, I was a little worried about his size. I was no virgin—even if Malphas *was*—but all it took was my determined mate turning his entire dick to shadow to make sure that he could fit that monster cock inside of me.

It worked, but that's not all that happened. We both discovered that he's even more sensitive when he slips from his solid form to his shadows. Not only that, but his pleasure increases mine exponentially. I climaxed almost immediately because I hadn't expected it to feel that amazing.

Since then, we've fucked countless times. I'm confident I can take him in any form, though I'd be lying if I said that—as an admittedly selfish lover sometimes—I don't immediately go off like a rocket when Mal gives me that shadow dick.

As I tease him with my mouth on his skin, I rub my thighs together to fight back my own arousal. I don't know why I even bothered to try. He might have been an innocent virgin when I first got my hands on him, but Mal is a seasoned lover now.

His thick fingers slip between our bodies. Like usual, his claws are completely turned to shadow. He'll never risk cutting me with their sharp points, though the sensation as he prods between my folds has me gritting my teeth in an attempt to keep from shouting out in need.

By the end of tonight, he'll have me howling. No doubt about that. But since he once had to explain to one of the clan hunters that the shriek he heard wasn't a predator with its kill, I'd rather wait to see if we can hold off on getting interrupted until *after* I come.

I've been dying for my mate since before the gold moon. I don't know what the hell I was thinking, doing a little foreplay when I got plenty of that last night. I want to be full of him. Stretched to the brink with his cock. I want to ride—

"Oh." My eyes flutter closed. "Yeah… okay. So maybe this was a good idea after all."

"Mm. Did you say something, my mate?"

I lick my bottom lip as Malphas slowly works a second finger inside of me to join the first. The best part is that, on an oversized shadow demon, one finger is almost as big as a human cock. Two? I'm getting that delicious stretch I wanted, and I *love* it.

The lava pool is only about four feet deep. It hits Mal around his middle, while I would be covered past my tits if it wasn't for his shadows. Still, I'm able to rise up on my tiptoes easily so that I can guide his fingers, making him fuck me with them as I sink back down.

I hiss.

He sucks in a breath. "Have I ever told you how beautiful you are when we're mating?"

Every damn time, but I never get sick of hearing it. "Thanks, babe."

He thrusts his fingers, going a little deeper. I clutch his arm, digging my nails past his shadows as his claws touch that spot inside of me that has me squealing.

"Beautiful," he rasps, repeating himself. "But you're even prettier when you come for me."

God, I love it when my sweet, formerly innocent mate talks dirty to me. It just means I taught him well, and since he could easily do just that if he keeps pumping his fingers like this, I know that I did. He's had years to perfect his technique, and forever to remind me why I decided to mate my monster in the first place.

I could easily give in. I could just let him touch me like this, knowing that he'll wait forever to find his own pleasure. To Mal, I always come first—and that includes actually *coming*.

But that's not what tonight is about. This is about reconnecting, and maybe I'm taking it too literally, but that means I want his cock inside of me instead of his fingers. I want him to pluck my clit with those wicked shadow claws while I bounce on his cock, a race to see which one of us will finish first.

Only one way to find out.

In a voice that's little more than a pleading whine, I tell him, "I need you, Mal. Not your fingers. Your cock. Won't you give it to me?"

His shudder is so forceful, he causes the lava pool to form slight waves. After one last pump, he pulls out his fingers. I'm only empty for a few seconds before he wraps one hand around me. With a gentle push against my ass, he lifts me up, guiding me to loop my legs around him.

With his height, we've had to find ways to make mating work. Whether he puts me on all fours and cages me in with his body until we line up perfectly, or he holds me aloft with his hand so that my pussy hits his groin and a simple tilt of my head means we can kiss as we fuck, it doesn't matter. I was meant to be his. He was meant to be mine. It might look weird on paper, but when you have two eager souls wanting to become one… yeah, it *works*.

His fingers stretching me out wasn't necessary. After going the entire gold moon without his dick to help me get through the worst of the lust, I've been waiting for him to impale me. I was probably slick enough to take his solid dick without any help, but between my lust, his practiced touch, and the remnants of the gold moon… as soon as his cock finds my entrance, he shoves and I'm fully seated on top of him.

Our first fuck tonight is fast. It's frantic. It's messy and not the least bit smooth. I could give a shit. Through our bond, I can sense just how desperate Malphas is for me. Same, big guy. He has me squirming almost instantly as he palms my ass, lifting me up and guiding me down so that I really am bouncing on top of him.

There are no words, dirty or not. It's pure animalistic rutting out in the gentle shadows of Sombra. So maybe there are some white eyes peering at us from the burnt woods at our back. And we're still near enough to Nuit that getting caught isn't just a possibility. It's something that adds to the excitement, even though no one will see me.

They'll see Mal, though, and my possessive side insists that they can't. His chest, sure. I love the way my name is inked on his skin, and when all of this prophecy nonsense is done, I'll go back to convincing

Mal that it's only fair that I get his name tattooed on me, too.

I know why he hesitates. Bond, remember? He thinks I could never love him… never *claim* him as much as he does me. He's wrong about that, obviously, but with our lives gone topsy-turvy since Alana was born, I decided to hold off on pestering him about something that's so clear.

Besides, why tell him when I can show him? And as I purposely ride him until he comes first, that's exactly what I do.

As Mal can't help but unload himself inside of me, the warmth of his jizz coupled with the reverential way he pants my name during his orgasm sets off mine. I squeeze him, continuing to ride out my climax as he shifts his hand, lovingly stroking my clit, just as I like. The last bit of stimulation rips the howl right out of my throat, and even if one of the villagers stumbles upon Mal's golden eyes gleaming boldly, the scent of our sex for once overpowering the rotten egg stink of this sulfurous world… I wouldn't change a damn thing about tonight.

Hey. He's my mate. My one true love. For god's sake, we have a kid. We fuck.

Get used to it.

As for me, when I can finally catch my breath again, I have only two words for my mate: "I win."

He brushes my hair out of my face, nuzzling my temple. "What's that?"

I shake my head, burying it alongside his thick throat. "Don't worry about it, babe. Besides, it doesn't matter. We're only just getting started."

Because another bonus to being a Sombra demon's mate?

When you're immortal, refractory periods? Who needs 'em?

Not me. I just need my mate. I need my daughter.

My happily-ever-after.

And I'm going to have it all, no matter what it takes.

MALPHAS

I t is the night after the gold moon, and my mate made up for a night of abstinence by allowing me to pleasure her until she nestled against my chest, falling asleep almost immediately after.

I stayed with her in the lava pool for a few moments more, just enjoying the feel of her naked skin against my shadows. I would've stayed forever in the content, quiet moment if I could, but I knew better.

For one, there are probably other mated couples who are eager to find privacy in one of the hidden pools. There are plenty of spawn who live in Nuit, but when it takes three long years for a demoness to grow her child inside of her, then at least a century before they're considered a mature demon, most bonded pairs only have one or two at a time before a gap of decades, if not centuries.

Sombra is a world of balance. Of superstition. Of magic, and our gods. They give us immortality and bless us with our one true mate, but while it isn't easy for a Sombra demon to die, our realm would be overrun if we conceived on every possible gold moon. To even the scales, when too many spawn are brought into our world, war happens. Famine happens. The predators in the shadows get hungry. And the weight of *forever* sometimes becomes too much to bear until demons with too many centuries to count simply fade away.

Not every demon is fortunate enough to find their one true mate. Some of us are patient. Some of us are determined. But when the years go by, and loneliness replaces hope, forever can seem like a punishment.

Death can be an escape.

I understand why a demon would give up. But when I hold my Shannon close, I also understand how far an honorable male would go to ensure that he held on tight to his forever…

I have more than just my mate now. And while Kennedy enjoys watching over Alana because she considers it 'practice' for when she has her child, to linger longer into the night when we should be home with our daughter… I held Shannon close, lifting her out of the pool before carrying her back to the village inside of my shadows.

After I laid her out on our bedding to sleep, I retrieved Alana from Loki and Kennedy's home. As always, my delightful daughter's gold-colored eyes lit up when she saw me. A demon child comes out larger than a human infant. Alana is four cycles old, four moons, but Shannon laughs and says that she looks closer to a toddler in her size and with her head of soft, pale curls twisting around her small horns.

She is still her mother's baby, though. She drinks from Shannon's breast, and won't speak for closer to a full Sombran year has passed. She sits up with a little help, and when she can climb, I know my mate and I will be in trouble.

For now, she cooed in delight as Kennedy handed her over to me. One hand landed on the side of my neck. The other grabbed for my nearest horn. I angled my head so she could clutch at the curve, not the point, while promising Loki and Kennedy that, when the time came and they needed their own privacy, Shannon and I would tend to their spawn.

Now both of my females are sleeping. Alana has her own room—the nursery, as Shannon calls it—right next to the quarters where her mother and I lie together. Just like the spare room we crafted over Turn the Page, I painted the walls in here to illustrate the gold moon shining over Sombra on one side, plus a scene from Main Street in Jericho on the other.

One of the burnt wood-workers in Nuit built a cradle to Shannon's exact specifications. I painted that as well, and Lilith's gift to Alana was a pillow-soft nest the clanmother sewed for our spawn. Once returned to our home, I placed Alana down inside the cradle, murmuring softly to her, patting her curls, waiting for her to fall asleep for the eve.

When she did, I returned to my mating quarters.

Shannon has barely moved from the curled-up position she was in when I slipped out to retrieve Alana. Despite constantly reminding me how hot Sombra is, she insists on sleeping with a sheet over her. One leg has slipped out from under it. Taking the hem in my claw, I drag it gently until she's fully covered.

I want nothing more than to join her. To lie on my side, acting like a utensil as I... not fork her... ah, *spoon* her. Holding her close, marveling at how fortunate I am to call this wee human female mine... but I can't.

The most I can allow myself is to crouch low, sliding my shadow claws through her hair. I shudder at the slight connection. Even asleep, our finalized bond thrums between us as my body instinctively recognizes the nearness of my mate.

My fingers stroke her ridge-free, colorless skin. The first time I touched my mate, I was shocked by the difference in our body temperatures. She'd seemed so erotically *cold*. The chill on my skin nearly had me spilling my seed then and there, even though my own skin was so hot, it seemed to burn her.

After the essence exchange, our bodies changed just enough that we're closer in temperature. I'm still warmer, she's still cool to the touch, and my tired body begins to stir from my fingertips brushing against her smooth skin.

Murmuring in her sleep, she turns into me as if giving me permission to continue stroking her gently.

My heart swells; so does the rest of me.

Tired as I am, I will never tire of her. The gods gave me this amazing female, and since we've been bonded, she's given me our spawn. I don't know what I have done in this existence to deserve such a gift, but I will fight for our family's future together.

I will fight Fate if I must.

I am not a hunter. I try, and with Nox teaching me, and Holden and Xoran letting me tag along when they seek out prey beasts to nab for the village, I've learned some defense skills. I will learn more, all to protect my spawn and my mate.

And if I must protect Shannon from herself, I shall.

That's why, when I sense someone approaching the back of our home, I reluctantly pull away from Shannon. My fingers already miss the feel of her soft skin. My cock urges me to ignore the summons. My brain knows that I cannot.

"I'll be right back, my flower," I murmur softly, then duck out of our quarters.

Alana was sleeping when I left her space. As I

move easily into the room again, I see she's pulled herself up, using the side of the cradle to sit and wait for me to retrieve her.

My clever daughter senses them, too.

Swooping her up, I'm not surprised that she quiets her coos as I hurry her down the stairs to the first floor of our home. As though she also knows that her mother needs her rest—and not to be worried by our monthly visitors—Alana is wide-eyed yet silent.

As I go, I check to see that the shadows I've woven to cover my body have held. In Sombra, when a demon doesn't plan on switching to their shadow form, he wears coverings created by the tanners and the seamstresses. Those without or who have need of fading to their shadow form... they create coverings from their shadows themselves.

I did that earlier when I went to retrieve Alana. There was no reason to change into linens or leathers when I wore shadows to the lava pool with my mischievous mate, and I didn't want to keep Loki and Kennedy waiting. Now? I check to make sure that my lower half is covered in shadows.

My top half? As always, I am pleased to show off the silver ink standing out against my deep red skin. **SHANNON**... I want all of Sombra to know that I'm proud to be claimed by my mate. Plus, if our visitors ever doubt who owns my heart... my loyalty? They only have to read the human letters on my chest to understand.

Once I'm sure that I'm decent enough to greet them, I open the back door and slip out into the night.

As busy as Nuit often is, we never meet near the village square. Someone would see us, and though I belong to this clan and can visit any part of it I wish, the two males who have come to see Alana belong to Sombra.

One is in his shadow form. His purple eyes shine out of the black shadows, the slightly hazy appearance making it difficult to recognize which of the doppelseers has come tonight.

The other male? He is the reason that we stand near the shadowy trees that back up to my home.

His colorless, white skin glows beneath the main moon almost as brightly as his unusual blue eyes. His crystalline crown twinkles softly, a hint of something delicate on a big, hard demon with sharp tusks and long, pale hair.

Duke Haures.

As the ruler of Sombra, he is welcome in every clan. Same with the powerful doppelseers. Apollyon would grovel in the ash to greet the duke if he knew he was here, but as we wait for some sign of the prophecy that was set into place as soon as the first-human, first-demon spawn was born, Duke Haures insists on keeping his cyclical visits between the four of us: the duke, the doppelseers, and me.

No. Five, including Alana.

From the moment she was born and Duke Haures realized that my daughter has no shadows inside of her, just like him, he's taken a special interest in her. He's convinced that she will develop a special gift as she ages. Haures is a bondmaster; he can sense, view, and break mate bonds with a whim. Even if she wasn't the spawn mentioned in the prophecy, he'd be curious to see what my halfling child might be able to do one day.

That is why he brings one of the doppelseers when he visits. Each one occurs the evening directly after the gold moon—which is why I knew to expect them tonight—and he insists on having the seer read my daughter. He told me he would do so immediately after she was born, and this is the fourth time he has returned with one of them instead of just having the doppelseers *see* from their charmed cabin.

Duke Haures believes the closeness will help them get a better read. It hasn't so far. Like their mate had done before, Alana is blocking Lucian and Damien. They see nothing of her future, or that of Sombra.

The fires of Sombra will be done…

Cupping Alana's head, holding her to me, I approach the two in silence.

Duke Haures never speaks. Probably because the duke can sense how nervous he makes me, or because he has nothing to say to a humble artist. I can't help but remember how he's always known—considering this prophecy is as old as Haures's reign as duke—that the first half-demon, half-human child born would trigger the possible end of his realm, and that he allowed it anyway.

Sometimes I wonder: is that why his first law as duke was to close the portals between the mortal realm and Sombra? Why it took nearly two thousand years for the matefinder spell to land in the hands of the human female meant for Haures? Why he's obviously refrained from mating on the night of the gold moon himself, instead waiting from his crystal throne in Mavro to see who would be the first Sombra demon with a human mate to bring a child into our worlds?

I don't know, and I can't ask the duke. I just stand there, continuing to match the quiet, as the doppelseer drifts forward, eyes locked on Alana.

He exhales softly. "No. There's no change," he murmurs, and that his voice has a rougher edge and no riddle to his words, I know it is Lucian who has come to Nuit tonight while Damien stayed behind with their fire-haired mate.

Duke Haures inclines his head, an unasked question.

Lucian shakes his. "I see red, and then there's green." He pauses for a moment. "Green eyes. Green Sombran eyes."

"Glaine?" I ask. He's the only green-eyed soldier who has any contact with Alana. No one else in Nuit is a member of the duke's guard except for him.

"No," Lucian echoes. "A soldier, yes, but none that currently serve Haures."

I look over at the duke. His expression is thoughtful, but still he stays silent as his gaze is drawn down to the curious spawn tucked against my chest.

She bubbles out a laugh, flexing her chubby little fist as if reaching out for something only she can see. It's not me. It's not the shadow demon or even the imposing duke.

It's something else, and I don't know what.

"This spawn will either save Sombra or doom it," whispers Lucian.

He's right.

And none of us know which, either.

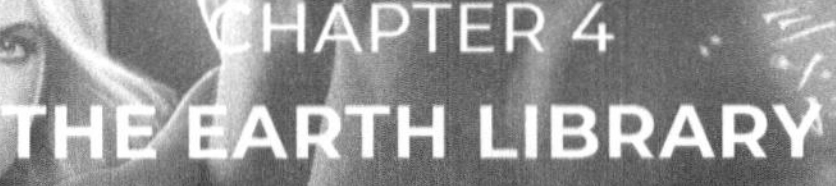

SHANNON

My whole adult life, I worked a 9-5 in an office. It paid decent enough that I could eventually live on my own without a roommate, though I wouldn't say it was my calling or anything.

And then, shortly after Kennedy read the *verus amor* spell and summoned Loki into her life, I found myself running the used bookstore where I first bought the *Grimoire du Sombra*. Somehow she ended up just giving it to me after she decided to stay in Sombra, and since I liked the idea of being my own boss—especially since she told us to take over her apartment over the shop, too, so it was like working from home with Mal hiding in his shadows whenever customers were around—I was like: fuck it. Let's do it.

It wasn't some big moneymaker. We made enough to keep the lights on and have a roof over our head and food in our bellies. It was enjoyable, though, and I loved it. Going back to run Turn the Page after a small vacation where I gave birth in Sombra was one thing I was looking forward to after Alana was born.

But, obviously, plans changed. Thankfully, I thought ahead early on in my pregnancy and paid the rest of the year's rent for the store and the apartment out of my 401k. I guess, part of me was preparing that something could happen and I might not be going back to Earth anytime soon.

It took two weeks into motherhood before I accepted that this is it. Unless we got the prophecy hanging over our heads out of the way, and Alana somehow developed some kind of glamour that made her look more human, returning to Jericho wasn't in the cards. By then, I was so stinking enamored with my baby as she was that I didn't even *want* her to be any different.

Though, if I could stop worrying about the damn prophecy, that would be *great*…

But that left the question: what would I do here? What would be my purpose? I'm the type of chick who needs one, and considering the best I can do when it comes to art is stick figures, it's not like I could be a clan artist with Malphas. However, Kennedy and me… we could run Turn the Page here in Sombra.

It was a crazy idea. Absolutely nuts.

I fucking *ran* with it.

Now, nearly four months after I went to Lilith and asked if we could have Loki conjure us a building to house as many books as the guys could slowly relocate from Turn the Page to Sombra, the Earth Library—or, as I call it, the EL—is the draw of Nuit. Open for a handful of hours, five days a week, it gives me something to do that isn't trying to convince Sombrans that it totally makes sense to measure time in days and weeks instead of just cycles, though they have a seemingly endless amount of it…

I didn't want to call it the Earth Library. I liked Kennedy's name for the store and was totally ready to name this one Turn The Page II. However, when the only people who could read English were me, Kennedy, and our mates, thanks to the essence exchange, it was inevitable that the villagers would smile and nod and say, "Oh, yes, the Earth library," and, well, the name just stuck.

Note that I say: *were*. Turns out, there are plenty of demons and demonesses who were curious to learn more about the mortal realm. And though Loki and Mal got their English courtesy of a magic download to their brains, between running the EL, taking care of Alana, and helping Kennedy prep for her baby's arrival, we've been teaching curious Sombrans and their mates how to both speak and read English.

So many of the demonesses have their own native language, with Sombra being one that we all can understand. Using that as the common tongue—and with Lilith's help as a clan teacher—we've made a *lot* of progress over the months. In fact, after only our second one 'in business', we already have at least two demons and four demonesses who are proficient enough in reading English that they are comfortable borrowing our books.

Because, *surprise*: immortal demons have a knack for picking up languages. I shouldn't have been so surprised about that. Kennedy's told me a bunch of times how, without Loki being able to do the essence exchange between them at first, they couldn't communicate since he only knew Sombran and she only knew English. Realizing that he wasn't letting her get away, she made it her purpose to teach Loki enough that they could communicate.

Of course, her intent had been to convince him to open a portal and bring her back to Jericho. By the time she tamed the feral beast enough to understand that, as his one true mate, he planned on keeping her for forever, she didn't *want* to go home again. She was fond of her beast, of how hard he worked to understand her, to honor her, and to please her.

He might've ended up healing enough from his fully demonic state to share his essence with Kennedy and take hers in return, becoming suddenly fluent in English, but she was impressed at how quickly he picked up as much of the language as he had.

With half of a bookstore filling up the EL, our students learned even *faster*.

No surprise to anyone who knows anything about the publishing industry, but nearly all of our new readers veer right to the romance section. And maybe that's because it's the section that Kennedy and I are the most familiar with, so we can make recommendations for their requests, but I think it's something more basic than that.

I mean, who doesn't love 'love', right?

It's funny, though. Back at home, it was hard to keep books in stock in the fantasy romance, paranormal, or even monster smut section. Here? The demonesses smile politely when I offer stories about the fae, wolf shifters, or—my personal favorite—shadow daddies while wondering if they could possibly read about cowboys or doctors or regular ol' average human dudes?

It only hit me much later that that makes so much sense. To a demoness, wouldn't a regular ol' average human dude *be* a fantasy?

It's been a slow day today. Alana cooed and babbled and waved at the two demons who came in to have a lesson with Kennedy and Lilith; I learned early on that while I'm great at talking about books and shelving the EL, I don't have the patience to teach. Kennedy left around lunch to eat with Loki while Lilith stayed to play with Alana until it was time for my baby to go down for a nap. Without any other lessons planned, she went home to check in with Apollyon before plotting her next lessons for the village's children.

Since I knew Mal was busy with a project today, I ate a couple of ash cookies—named because they're baked in the ash, not made from it… though their less than sweet taste makes me wonder sometimes—and stuck around the EL to see if anyone wanted to browse our stacks.

We only have eight. Eventually, I'm hoping that we can relocate *all* of Turn the Page here, but we didn't want to do that so quickly. Mainly because I want to keep the shop locked up tight in Jericho until my lease runs out, and if someone notices that the store's been closed for months and books are moving overnight without anyone seeing who is doing it, that might beg a couple of questions. Last thing I need is the Jericho PD shutting down Turn the Page and closing the one entrance into Jericho that we know is safe for Mal and Loki to pop in and out without any human possibly catching sight of them.

Still, it's a start. And since one of the stacks has a couple of Sombran books that Lilith donated, we have something for everyone, even if we're the *Earth* Library.

In the farthest corner of the library, I have a handmade playpen that was a gift from Kennedy and Loki when it became obvious we were going to stay. During some of the many trips back and forth in the early days following Alana's birth, Malphas brought back everything we had accumulated that a halfling baby might need. Cloth and disposable diapers, bottles, nipples, clothes, blankets, baby-safe dishware and toys, plus some of the bigger items: a pack-and-play, a changing table, and a car seat. While I'm too bougie to go completely demon—though I can't complain that the trash systems… similar to the waste system… in Sombra makes disposing of dirty diapers a breeze—there's something sweet about using some-thing that was *made* for her.

Like her cradle, and this playpen, and all the blankets that the kind seamstresses made for her.

She's sitting on one now, showing off how advanced she is. Her thumb is tucked between her budding fangs, her golden eyes pretty and happy and content as I read one of the children's books we have to her during the downtime.

Just when I'm thinking that I can close up an hour or two early and snuggle with Alana at home, the door opens, letting in a rush of hot air.

I glance over at the front of the library, smiling when I recognize the demoness entering it. "Hey, Yvette," I say in English. She insists so she can prac-tice her grasp on it. "What's up?"

Yvette is from Brille Rouge. She's mated to Ferron, one of the best cooks in Nuit. When he shares his meat stew with us, so it's delicious, I don't even ques-tion what the chunks might actually be.

The first time I said that, the adorable demoness paused and glanced up at the ceiling. She knows better now that it's just a human saying, and in response, she waves.

"Hello, Shannon. Alana. It is good to see you both."

She has a slight accent since English is so new to her, and Sombran isn't her first language, either. Like me, Ferron gave her his essence and his language, but there's always a tiny hint that she's not from here. You could figure that out from her gleaming pink eyes, dark brown skin, short white horns, and curly thick hair, of course, but the accent helps.

In fact, talking to Yvette makes me wonder what I sound like when I speak in Sombran. Something harsh, like a New Yorker who isn't quite fluent in Spanish but passable at it, perhaps. I'm sure it's nowhere near as lyrical as someone like Mal or maybe Damien, but since everything I hear and speak sounds like English to me, I'll never know unless I ask.

And if I ask Mal, he'll just smile and tell me that my voice is music to his pointed ears, the big sap.

"You, too." After double-checking that Alana is content with her teether, I get up and approach Yvette. "What can I do for you?"

"I come for more cock book," she says pleasantly.

It takes everything I have not to burst out laughing. "What was that?"

Sombra demons have ridges over their noses. Brille Rouge demons have skin with a slightly bumpy texture. As she scrunches up her face, her features join together, looking more rock-like. "Was my human not good?"

"Oh, no, no, sweetie. Your, um, human is very good." Switching to Sombran, I tell her, "I just wanted to make sure that I understood. You want a book about *cock*?"

"About mating, yes," she answers in the native language. "I finished one about a man who liked to chop wood and lie with his mate. It was very entertaining. I would like more like that."

"Lumberjacks," I tell her, slipping back into English because there's no direct Sombran translation for that. No surprise. All they have are burnt trees, and if I start to wonder where we get oxygen from when this is the least green world I've ever heard of, I make sure to drop it real quick before it feels hard to breathe all of a sudden. "I think I have more of those."

As I move toward one of the many romance stacks, she follows behind me. "Sometimes I flip through the pages, searching for the human word. For 'cock'. Then I know I've found the right scenes." Preening a little, she adds, "I read them to Ferron before bed. It gives him ideas and helps him learn to speak human. Then he says dirty things to me as he…" She pauses, glancing around. When she sees that no one else has entered our library behind her, she giggles, then says, "*fucks* me. That's right, yes?"

Another muffled chuckle from me at the English word mixed in with Sombran. "Perfect, Yvette."

Since she seems pretty clear on what she wants—and I made sure to assure her that I don't mind that she's held onto the last book a little longer for 'inspiration'—I search through the shelves, letting out a soft 'ah-ha' when I find *The Woodsman's Secret Bride*. That sounds right up her alley.

"Here you go."

She takes it reverentially between her curved claws. "Thank you. I am very curious about this woodsman's mate."

"Well, you tell me all about her when you're done."

And maybe keep what happens between you and Ferron to yourself…

Yvette grins and promises that she will. I wave her off, check on Alana again because motherhood is a one-way trip to anxiety hell, then turn to the ledger where I keep track of who borrows what book from the library.

It doesn't take long for me to jot down the title and Yvette's name, but when I'm putting my pen I had Mal bring, too, down on the page, I glance up to see a demoness standing a few feet away from Alana's playpen.

I don't know everyone in Nuit on sight just yet. For sure, the Soleil demoness—with features like Lilith's, only without any of her warmth—is not a member of the EL or our English lessons. She might be the mate of one of the older hunters, but I won't lie: I only think that because the sneer of disgust I caught on her face is the same as the one he gives me when I'm strolling around the village square with Alana.

My back goes right up even as the demoness works to smooth out her features.

Okay. I've made the best of it. I love living with Mal, and I've made good friends. Kennedy, Lilith, Billie when she's here, the other human girls who visit, even Yvette. The EL gives me something to do, and I thought that the villagers would get used to me in time.

They never had a problem before. They all seem to adore Kennedy. And yet, ever since I've tried to really integrate into the community, I get this vibe that they suddenly want me gone.

Good luck. I'll do anything to keep my daughter safe and my family together, whether these mean girls —these mean *demonesses*—want me to or not.

So, pulling a customer service smile to my face, though I keep my eyes hard, I nod at her. "Welcome to the Earth Library."

She startles, as though she didn't expect me to speak. Hell. I even purposely used Sombran so as not to really rub in my humanness so I don't know what freaked her out.

Something did, though. Without a word in response, she throws one last look at Alana, then turns on her heels, hurrying out the door.

I think I know how she got inside the EL without me noticing before. She must've slipped in as Yvette left because right as *she* storms out the door, Kennedy sidles in a second ahead of the door closing shut again.

I say, sidle… poor chick basically waddles as Freya —her pet squirrel-cat—chitters at her feet. The shadow animal throws herself up, rubbing Kennedy's calf, before bounding over to the low playpen to visit with Alana.

Heading toward the check-out counter, jerking her thumb at the door, Kennedy asks me curiously, "What was Nita's hurry?"

I wish I knew, Ken. I wish I knew.

SHANNON

I stew over the demoness's reaction all the way through dinner.

Draven is one of the ash field farmers. His mate, Collidia, is an excellent baker who has been pregnant the entire time I've known Mal. Because of the whole 'demonesses being knocked up for *three years*' thing, she must've just started showing when I first met her. Now, it's a race to see who will pop first: Kennedy or Collidia.

In Sombra, there is no real concept of money; at least, not when you live in one of the smaller villages like Nuit. Coins and wealth exist in larger cities, especially the capital, but, when you're a part of a clan, you work together to survive.

There's a casual barter system that we use, similar to the suburban habit of knocking on your neighbor's door for a cup of sugar. If you need something, ask around, and you'll eventually find someone who will help out. Either for a price now or a favor later, it's amazing how the system works.

The farmers and the hunters share their food. A handful of villagers prepare it—like baking bread or ash cookies—and pass it out among the rest of us. Collidia and Draven are part of that provider circle. That's why, after Collidia heard about the beautiful murals that Malphas painted on Alana's nursery walls and mentioned she might like one for her own baby, my mate didn't even hesitate. For the last week or so, whenever he could spare the time, he's been painting her walls.

And, no, that's not a euphemism. The best thing about locking down a Sombra demon? They are fanatically loyal. Seriously. A line-up of naked models wouldn't turn Malphas's head. If anything, he might wonder if they didn't have clothes before asking if they needed him to use his shadows to cover them up.

After all, us humans have such a puritanical view of nudity. At least, that's the impression I gave him when, directly after I accidentally summoned him, I pointed out his obviously naked body and asked him to cover up. I mean, how was I supposed to know he was in the middle of taking a bath when I fooled around with the *Grimoire du Sombra* and read the true love spell?

Then again, how did I know my true love would be an immortal shadow demon from another realm? I laugh now to remember how I was hoping it might give me the nerve to ask Derek at The Beanery out on a date. He was cute, but Mal… yeah. Fate definitely did her job on *that* one.

Even as pissed off as I am that that demoness openly sneered at Alana, I can appreciate how gorgeous my mate is as he finishes the stew that Collidia sent him home with as a 'thank you' for completing her mural. And maybe if another demon —a young hunter this time—didn't shy away from me and Alana as I carried her home earlier tonight, I might've been able to let it go.

Might've been… nah. I'm Shannon freaking Crewes. When have I ever been able to let *anything* go?

I do, however, manage to wait until after he clears our crystal table from the dinner mess and I've finished feeding Alana before letting her curl up in my lap and cuddle. Usually, I put her down after her last feeding, but tonight I want to hold her a little longer.

Is it because of me? Is it because she's half-human? Since Haures decreed that we don't discuss the prophecy with the rest of the villagers, it can't be that. I never got the vibe that Nuit was full of anti-human bigots, but today was my tipping point.

I'm sitting on the couch in our designated 'living room', Alana still on my lap, when I finally decide that I have to say something to Malphas about it.

"So, the weirdest thing happened today, babe," I begin. "And by 'weird', I mean super fucking rude."

His brows furrow. "Is something wrong, my flower?"

He can say that.

"It was the EL. One of the demonesses came in… not one of my regulars, but someone else. It doesn't really matter who because, welp, this isn't the first time it's happened."

Mal moves over to the couch, sinking down next to me. "What has happened?"

A small shrug as I try not to let my annoyance turn to outright anger. Mal doesn't deserve it. "I had just finished up with Yvette when I saw her. She was standing over Alana's playpen, staring at our girl. But, like, not with curiosity or interest. She kinda looked… disgusted."

That's the word for it, and why it rubbed me the wrong way. Who the hell looks at a baby like that?

Mal gulps. "Oh."

Oh?

What does he mean, oh?

"Mal?"

He sighs. "I had hoped that, over the many centuries, my people had given up their silly superstitions. That they would understand that, with you as her wonderful mother, our spawn might be different from the others."

Hang on.

"So, it *is* my fault? They don't like her because she's half-human? Because I thought people in Sombra were a little more open-minded than that, too."

And why did I? Because Malphas seemed to marvel over the fact that a human was his mate. I've heard from Kennedy how some unmated demons made wishful comments to Loki that, one day, they might have a human female like he does. And, of course, the leader of its realm even treasures his human duchess. True, he keeps her tucked away and out of sight, but Susanna Benoit is Amy's aunt. She's told me how much Haures has obsessively cared for his mate over the last fifty years that they've been bonded. Humans are the stuff of legends, not monsters creeping into Sombra…

At least, that's what I *thought*. Was I wrong?

Mal takes in a breath, releasing it slowly through his nose. He worries his fangs against his bottom lip, hand lifting to nervously stroke his horn.

I arch an eyebrow. I know Mal. Sure, I got a download about him from the essence exchange after we first met, but over the years that we've been together, I've learned everything I need to know about my demon myself. I don't need to rely on his essence when I have my own memories and experiences that I've had with him.

So, yeah, he's nervous. I can sense the anxious emotion trickling down our bond, and though I could tap into his essence and figure out what's going on here, that's not how a solid, trusting relationship works. We need communication, and, damn it, I'm gonna sit here and wait until my mate wants to communicate with me.

I wait.

He gulps.

Cradling Alana's back with my left hand, my baby blissfully unaware of the tension brewing between her parents, I use my right hand to casually stroke Mal's thick thigh.

I wait some more.

He sighs. "I am so sorry, my Shannon. If I led you to think that it's her human blood the others are wary of… no. It's not that. It's her lack of shadows. Sombran demons are born with shadows. Our Alana wasn't."

You know something? He's right. That's exactly what I *did* think. Of course it is. Why would I ever think anything was wrong with my adorable, perfect daughter? One part Mal, one part me, visible proof of our love—and, well, our sex life—and the most adorable baby I've ever seen in my life… it couldn't be her.

But Malphas just admitted that it is. All because she… what?

"Who says she doesn't have shadows?"

Mal reaches out, trailing one of his claws along Alana's chubby cheek. "That she was born with colorless skin does."

Bullshit. "Dude, I'm white. You're red. She's basically pink. Come on, Mal. You're an artist. That's basic color mixing."

"I wish it were so. But Sombra demons have very strong characteristics." Characteristics? It's not a perfect translation, but I think what he's trying to discuss is genetics as he adds, "She was always meant to take after me more than you. With her eyes and her horns and her shadows. But Alana… she has my eyes, she has tiny horns, but… she has no shadows."

Okay. Fine. Let's say her having no shadows is some kind of big deal that I didn't know about. "And they're really going to give her the stink-eye because part of me won out? I mean, look. She's got my blonde hair. After all, I *am* her mother."

He twirls one of her curls around his finger. "And there hasn't been a better one in all of existence."

I roll my eyes. "Now you're just trying to sweet-talk your way out of this conversation."

"No," he insists. "Any demoness who gave birth to a child born without their shadows wouldn't love them like you love Alana. They wouldn't care for them." His face shadows, and since he's a shadow demon in his solid form, that's pretty impressive. "They would be left on the edge of the deepest, darkest shadows of our world to... to..." He shakes his head. "To *perish*."

What?

No.

That doesn't make *sense*. "Okay. Let's backtrack before I lose my ever-loving shit here. You're telling me that if a baby is born like Alana... they abandon them? They... kill them?"

That's what Mal means by 'perish'?

"The shadows take them in the end," he murmurs softly. "In fact, only one demon in our history has ever been left to the shadows and survived."

It doesn't take a Sombran historian to know who *that* is. Like, gee, who is the only Sombra demon I've ever seen without the red skin, the black hair, and a shadow form? I just figured that Haures was too high and mighty to ever be vaguely hidden in the dark, so he always stayed in his striking white-colored solid form instead.

But that's not the reason, is it? It's because he doesn't *have* a shadow form...

And, if Mal is right, neither does Alana. I just... I guess I thought it would come as she got older. But he has a point. In the last four months, she's never shown that she has any other form than the one she's in now. Pale and solid, and a death sentence to some of these villagers.

What the fuck am I supposed to do? It's bad enough that my sweet Alana has the weight of the prophecy hanging over her innocent head. I've come to terms with the fact that I can't even bring her home, introduce her to my parents, and show her off to my friends, like Tori and Chris. But now he's telling me that she'll always be an outcast in Sombra, too? And that, deep down, they probably all wonder why we haven't booted her to the shadows already?

Fuck, no.

I grit my teeth. "Thanks for finally telling me, Mal."

"It wasn't supposed to matter," my big demon says insistently. "She is our spawn. I love her with all of my heart, just like I adore you, my flower. I never wanted you to worry about this when it's clear that neither one of us would change a thing about Alana. If some demons don't see the magic in her, that is their concert, not ours. Besides, Duke Haures has her under his protection. While he rules Sombra, no one will harm Alana. He vowed it."

That's news to me. "He did? When?"

I see the panic flash across his strong features, feel the way his heart jumps all the way from the other side of our bond, and I know that, whatever Mal says next, I'm not gonna be happy with what it is.

"When he came to visit her a cycle after she was born. He hasn't said anything else during the last few visits, but he's given his word. And the duke will not go back on it."

Yeah, see… that's not what I'm focusing on…

Wow.

Okay.

I was right just now, but I think I was definitely wrong before. Maybe Malphas *does* deserve my anger after all.

"What?" The word is quiet so I don't upset Alana, but there's enough heat to it that Mal has to know he pissed me off. "Are you telling me that he's been coming to see our baby, and you're *just* letting me know?"

I didn't want to upset Alana, but she is as intuitive as her father. She lets out a soft coo, head swiveling to look at Mal, then me.

I bounce her gently, waiting for my mate to come clean.

"He visits her after every gold moon," Malphas finally admits. "It's late when he comes. You're usually sleeping, my mate. I didn't want to disturb you."

"And Alana?" I ask through gritted teeth.

His glowing eyes dim. "I always hope she will sleep through the meeting. It's very quick. Mere minutes, if that."

That didn't answer my question. "Mal."

There's only a hint of a glow now. "She wakes up," my mate confesses. "As though she knows they've come to see her, she never sleeps until they're gone."

Smart girl.

Her father, though? I'm not so sure.

Jumping up from my seat, needing a little space, I begin to pace around the room with Alana. "Are you kidding? You really thought I'd rather sleep than let the two of you face Haures alone? Did you forget he wanted to put you in a dungeon for not fucking me fast enough?"

Malphas winces. "My mate—"

"Zip it," I snap. "You were trying to protect me. I get it. But don't you understand that, as your mate, it's my job to protect you, too?"

"You always have—"

No. I've *tried*. Just like I would've done the same for Alana if I had been given the choice. "We're a family, Mal. It's you and me and Alana against the world. In Earth… in Sombra… it's us. You don't hide things from me, whether you're doing it *for* me or not. Got it?"

He gets up, inching closer to me. "I vow it."

That calms me a little. Sombra demons take their vows super seriously. If he vows it now, he won't go back on his word. Just like, if the duke really did vow to protect Alana, their gods will hold him to it.

Maybe that's not such a bad thing. Having the ruler of Sombra invested in keeping Alana safe if only because of her supposed destiny… I should be happy to take all the help I can get.

Plus, the next time someone sneers at my daughter, I'll just have to tell them that Duke Haures wouldn't like it…

I exhale.

Malphas approaches me hesitantly. "Are you mad?"

That's the thing. I'm not really *mad*. Disappointed, yes, but how can I be mad when he was only doing what he thought was best for me and Alana? "No," I tell him. "Not really. But if you ever do something like that again—"

I don't honestly know how I was going to end my baseless threat. Probably with something I wouldn't actually mean, but it doesn't really matter because, suddenly, I'm distracted by two very seemingly impossible things happening at the exact same moment.

For the first time that I've seen, Alana throws back her head and cries. It's a loud, piercing screech that is like a knife to my heart. Her cries quickly turn inconsolable, gasping sobs that have her face becoming as red as a full-blooded Sombra demon.

That's enough to shock me. I guess I got used to such a well-tempered baby that part of me thought she would never cry.

But as I instinctively go into 'mom' mode, trying my best to comfort her while Mal hovers beside me, eager to help, I see something on the window that I *know* I've never seen before.

Droplets of water. Honest-to-god *rain* droplets.

My breath catches in my throat.

Panic has me rushing over to the glass, peering through it, making sure I'm not imagining what I'm seeing.

I'm not.

"Mal…" My voice is quiet. Shaky. Alana's cries drown it out, but he hears me anyway as I whisper, "It's *raining*."

CHAPTER 6
RAIN

MALPHAS

It's raining.

It's raining in Sombra. Not the hazy, barely there mist of moisture that is enough to water the ash farmers' fields before evaporating, but a constant fall that reminds me of my time on Earth.

Worse, as the rain pours, my child cries.

Alana doesn't cry. She giggles and coos and, when she's hungry, she makes a demanding sound for her mother's breast, but she has never cried that I've known. Not real tears such as the ones streaking down her cheeks as Shannon rubs her back, attempting to soothe our spawn even as she stares out the window.

To keep the Sombra heat out, the glass is closed. When Shannon and I first decided that we would stay in Nuit after Alana was born, the window was the first concession I made so that my home became ours. Like the window in the apartment that allowed us to look out over Jericho, she likes to peer out into Sombra.

She calls it being nosy. I'm not sure what her nose has to do with anything since her human senses can't scent anything through the glass, but if it makes Shannon happy to have a window in our front room and upstairs where Alana sleeps, I was happy to make one for her with my own two hands.

The glass opens. I created our window to be just like the one in New York, another slice of the human world that I gave to Shannon in Sombra. Because I don't know how to get Alana to stop crying, I focus on the window instead.

Sliding it open just enough that I can reach outside, I let the rain land on my skin.

Sombra demons are heat. As scalding as the raindrops are, they sizzle and evaporate the instant they touch my flesh. But they burn, a sensation that I've never experienced before. From a young age, spawn know to stay away from the lava pits if they can't control their shadows. I've never touched fire unless I've first faded to my second form—

No. That's not true. When my Shannon summoned me to her human world, she'd known enough about demonkind to create a protective circle that trapped me. I could break through it, but doing so, I burned away some of my essence—and my hand. Then, before Shannon understood that Sombra demons are truly *shadow* demons, she tried to leave me. The gods don't allow that until a bond is finalized, or it's broken.

I burned then, too.

But it didn't hurt. Not like the tiny droplets that sear my skin wherever they hit do. Almost instinctively, I let my shadows out. The next raindrop falls through the edge of them, finding my corporeal form inside.

That feels *worse*. Like an itch and a sting and an ache all at the same time.

I wince, and Shannon moves into me.

"Mal? What's going on?"

She sounds so uncertain. It's a tremor down our bond, and I want nothing more than to tell her that all will be well.

But it is raining, and Alana still cries.

"I must check with Apollyon," is what I say instead.

The clan leader will know what to do. He can have Loki use his magic to send a message to Duke Haures if he doesn't already know. The rain… is this it? The prophecy unfolding?

The gods help us all if it is.

I loop my arm around Shannon, my shadows surrounding my mate and my child for a moment before I drop a kiss to her hair. Then, releasing her while staying in my mist, I zip through one of the holes built into the ceiling. Through the first floor, then the second, I go until I land in the middle of the village square, my shadowy feet managing to sink into the damp ash.

The ash in Sombra has never been so wet before.

The volcanic surface of our world reacts to the rain. It spits and sizzles, the same way it did when it touched my skin, while the air blooms with a foul stink.

It's empty. The village square, that is. Though, as a mere clan artist, my house has always been more basic than those belonging to the clan leader, the hunters, the farmers, and the weavers, I built it from the ash up with my future mate in mind. It's humble yet sturdy, and it has the best view of all of Nuit.

From our porch, we can see the expanse of the entire village before the boundaries fade to shadows. It's another reason why I loved the idea of adding the window. That way, we can see the village from the comfort of our home.

Nuit is one of the smaller villages in Sombra, but we are a close clan because of it. We trade, and we help each other; though I had expected their wariness when it came to Alana's differences, it hurt me all the same because the demons in our village were the only kin I had after my mother and father moved on themselves centuries ago.

It is always busy, even when the moons rise and the shadows darken. The ash farmers tending to their crops. The hunters going out for nocturnal prey. Bonded mates enjoying the lava pools like my Shannon and I did… but not this eve.

I see no one. I hear no one. Though lights flicker in some of the smaller windows I spy through the rain, all of the villagers are hunkered down in their homes.

No one else is here to watch the rain fall. Do they even know the skies have opened up? That the prophecy might be unfolding before my very eyes?

Do they—

Behind me, I hear a door open. Glancing over my shoulder, I turn in time to notice that it's from my house. With a hint of defiance, my mate steps out onto the porch.

"Woof," Shannon says, cradling Alana to her chest with one hand. With the other, she shoves her fingers under her nose. "It usually stinks like rotten eggs out here, and I thought I got used to it, but add the rain to it and… shit, that's nasty."

"Shannon, my flower. I thought you were going to stay inside."

She snorts. I'd like to think it's because of the stench, but I know my mate better than that.

Especially when she says, "Don't know why you'd think that, big guy. Just because I can't go *poof* and fly outside, my fingers work just fine when it comes to opening the door." Shannon moves toward the edge of the porch. "Legs work, too."

"I wanted you to stay inside where it's safe," I try to tell her. "This rain isn't like Earth rain."

Still clutching Alana tightly, my mate ignores me as she holds out her free hand, testing the rain.

My heart jumps into my throat. "Shannon—"

"I don't get the big deal. It's warm, but it's not acid rain, Mal. Besides, I'm not the Wicked Witch of the West. I won't melt."

I gasp. "Is that even possible?"

"In Oz, maybe."

Oz? That's a relief. I thought that she meant Earth, and though I lived with her for years in her human realm, I never once worried that my mate would disintegrate if she got caught out in the rain.

Still… "I don't want it to cause you any pain."

Even standing here in my shadows, it is an annoyance every time one of the droplets hits me.

Shannon scoffs. "It's rain. I'll be…" Her expression twists back into one of unease. "Wait— does it hurt *you*?" I don't even get the chance to answer before she scrabbles backward, hurrying so that she's standing under the ash-awning on the porch. Normally, it protects anyone near the house from scattered ash, but for the first time in my existence, it blocks out the falling rain. "Alana is half-demon. What if it hurts *her*?"

What if she is the reason it rains?

I immediately regret my fleeting suspicion. The looming prophecy has weighed down on me. It's led to a fight with my beloved mate, and my daughter's first tears. But whether or not it is because of the prophecy… it doesn't matter. I'm the only one to blame for upsetting both Shannon and Alana.

"I won't let anything hurt her," I vow.

Shannon calms, though she stays on the porch. "I know, baby. I know. But I don't want anything to hurt you, either. Come over here. You want to talk to Apollyon? Either he comes here, or you can wait until it stops raining. But, please, don't walk away from us, Malphas."

I would *never*.

I surge forward, slipping on the slick ash with my first step. In my solid form, I can control my body better. In my shadows, I could float—but it doesn't even occur to me. I just want to get to my family, and running toward them is instinctive.

I don't fall. Recovering my balance, I bound up the stairs. Once there, I surround them again.

"Never," I say aloud, cementing my vow. "You never have to fear me leaving your side, my mate."

Shannon leans into my embrace. "Thanks, baby. I just… it's been rough."

And I didn't make it any easier by hiding the truth behind why some of the villagers would treat her as though she didn't belong. It's no wonder she began to think it had everything to do with her being a human. On Earth, so many people hate others for trivial differences. The color of their skin.

Who they love. Whether they are male or female or neither.

Sombra demons welcome all. My whole existence, mortal females were legendary. I am the envy of many of my fellow Sombrans because the gods granted me Shannon as my mate. She *is* my mate; that makes her a Sombran, too, now. Just like when a Sombra demon finds his mate in a Soleil demoness, or one from Brille Rouge. Without finding our forevers in a different world, we might always be lonely.

So, no… it's not because of who Alana's mother is.

It's how similar my child is to the fearsome Duke Haures—born in a shadow realm, with Sombran blood and the glow in her eyes, but no shadows at all —that has more than a few villagers in Nuit treating her poorly enough that it upset my Shannon. And what made it worse? Is that I suspected that would be my poor spawn's fate from the moment she was born… and I never told Shannon.

I wanted to shield her. To protect her.

Instead, I failed her.

Not again.

Never again.

"I am here. I will always be wherever you are."

It may not be the mate's promise, but it is my vow to my one true mate, and I mean every word of it.

Luckily, she does not doubt me. "I know, and— oh. Oh, Mal, thank fucking God." Shannon clicks her tongue, rubbing the back of Alana's head as relief washes over her. "She stopped crying. Oh, good, good girl. Mommy's got you."

As glad as I am to hear that she's succeeded in soothing our spawn, something pulls my attention out to the village square. I blink, then I stare.

The rain has finally stopped, too.

SHANNON

Five minutes. The whole freak rainstorm lasted maybe five minutes.

I don't even know if anyone else in Nuit is aware it happened. It was the weirdest thing. For the first time since I've been in the village, no one else was around in the square. And, sure, Nuit isn't anything like New York, where the city never sleeps. It's just that I expected to see someone, *anyone* else rushing outside to watch the rain fall.

It's like rubbernecking. You can't help yourself. You just have to stare. I'm telling you, if lava started falling from the sky back home, my nose would be plastered to the window. And when it stopped as suddenly as it started, I'd be one of the first ones out the door.

After Mrs. Winslow, of course. That old biddy might've risked getting petrified to be the first one to know what's going on, but that's my point. Human and demon nature aren't *that* different. Even if most of the villagers have no idea that the prophecy about Alana involves a rain that puts out Sombra's fires for once and for all, erasing its shadows at the same time, it's gotta be something unusual to break up what has to be the monotony of immortality.

Nope. As though they all had a nice sleep and woke up having no clue what Mal and Alana and I witnessed last night, everyone is going about, business as usual today.

I barely slept at all. Seeing that I was shaky as fuck, Mal gave up on going to see Apollyon last night once Alana settled down and the rain just… stopped. He looped his arm around me, turning solid so that he had a firm hand to guide me inside. I held tightly to Alana, refusing to even entertain putting her down again until Mal gently pointed out that she had fallen asleep.

My mate eased our baby out of my arms, laying her out in her crib. The two of us watched her sleep for a few seconds before I let him lead me to bed.

He curled his big body around me, absently stroking my sunflower tat on my upper arm while I confessed that I didn't believe it could really happen. I had tricked myself into believing that the prophecy was nonsense. That, even if it *was* real—and I wasn't just taking the doppelseers' word for it—the prophecy could take centuries before it unfolded.

The Sombrans are immortal, right? Who said that this responsibility belonged to a four-month-old baby? Why couldn't Alana be, like, six hundred before the rain came?

Malphas lay there with me, letting my insecurities and fears spill from me in a panicked rant. His touch never slowed, and I realize why when he reminded me that he was once the subject of a prophecy by another, less powerful clan seer. When he was much younger, he was told that he would find his one true mate in a female full of magic that blooms in the sun. He never knew what that meant—mainly because Sombra is a demon realm with two moons and no visible sun—but when he took my essence and got that download of English into his brain, he knew. From the moment I told him my ink was of a sunflower, he *knew* that his prophecy had come true. Up until then, it didn't even occur to him that he would be meant for a human woman since he interpreted 'sun' to mean the gold moon and the seer didn't correct him, and I clung to the idea that Alana's prophecy could be misunderstood, too.

Even if it isn't, my point still stands. Mal was over a *thousand* when he found me. We should have more time.

And maybe we do.

Just like I soothed Alana, my mate made it his job

to calm me down. He reminded me that rain isn't impossible in Sombra, just not common, and while it usually evaporates before it hits the ash, it might all have been a fluke.

To be honest, it wasn't the rain that had me so worked up. It's easy to latch onto it and blame the weather when watching my daughter cry real tears for the first time messed me up. Add that to learning that Malphas had kept Haures's monthly visits to see Alana from me, and I didn't know what to think. I understand why he did it. In his sweet way, Mal is as protective of me and our baby as I am of him and Alana. From the duke's experiences, Mal guessed that some of the villagers might side-eye Alana because of her lack of shadows.

I just… it might've been nice if he told me.

Now that I *do* know, that's an easy problem to fix. You don't like my baby? Fuck you. It's as simple as that. There are plenty of villagers who dote on her and enjoy having humans around to add a little spice and variety to Nuit. For those that don't, they can stay away from the EL, me, and my family.

Because Shannon is in Sombra for good, and now that there's no denying that the prophecy isn't something to mess around with, I'm going to do anything I can to save this world. Not for them. Like I said, fuck 'em. But Sombra is Mal's home. Alana's, too. We have forever to show the bigots the mistakes they made in doubting *my* daughter.

Hell, I'm a petty bitch. Nothing is better than showing the haters that I'm thriving and surviving.

So, forgiving Mal and telling him that we're in this together, I finally managed to get a few hours down before Alana woke up, cooing and waiting for her morning feeding.

Mal got her for me, hovering as though concerned she would start crying again—and that the rain would start shortly after. Considering he confessed that he believed the two incidents were related last night, I'm a little worried myself, but Alana is in a fantastic mood.

And honestly? It's tough to hang on to my foul, anxious one when she's around.

Malphas seemed happier, too, for the first part of the day. Through breakfast and our morning family time, I could sense him getting withdrawn until he finally stood up from the table and told me it was time to go see Apollyon.

I almost insisted on going with him. I wouldn't mind talking to Lilith since I haven't had a chance to bring up the whole 'villagers being dicks to Alana' thing that started this whole mess. However, if it turns out that Alana's tears *are* the reason it rained, I feel a little better about keeping her at home in case Apollyon decides to narc on me and get in touch with Haures.

Then again, now that I know he's been making

these monthly visits, I wouldn't be surprised if he's already preparing to stop by today...

Luckily for me, we might've dodged a bullet. Apollyon acknowledged that he knew about the storm, but since it was over almost as soon as it began—to the clan leader, maybe, since it seemed like an eternity to me while it was happening—he decided that it was just bad luck rather than the prophecy kicking into gear.

Did he report it to the duke? Probably, but if they're all acting like everything's hunky-dory, I'll go along with it, too...

"Oh," Malphas says to me, drawing my attention back to him and out of my own head, "I almost forgot to mention it. On my way back from meeting with Apollyon, I saw Dagon."

"Dagon?" I echo.

"And Sammael."

Wait... "Sammael? Not Sierra?"

He understands my confusion immediately. "Ah. His mate. No, she's here as well. She's visiting with Azazel." Then, anticipating my next question, he adds, "Hope has gone with her. Sammael assured me that he and his mate have not changed their mind about having spawn of their own, but Hope has come with Sierra for..." He pauses, wrinkling his forehead so that his ridges are more pronounced. "Mortal support."

"Moral support," I correct with a slight tease.

"Smart, you know, bringing another chick in with her. It's probably easier for the healer to check her v-jay out without her protective mate growling softly somewhere behind him."

"I apologize, my mate. I didn't like another male seeing your cunt."

"Don't be sorry. I like that side of you." I raise my eyebrows. "Turns me on."

Mal's eyes flare like a yellow traffic light. "Where is Alana?" he rumbles.

"Down for a nap. She should be sleeping for the next hour or so."

His lips curve, his fangs so incredibly erotic as he widens his smile. "I don't have any painting to do for the afternoon. Are you heading to the library?"

After yesterday, I decided I need a small break from the EL. "Nope."

He moves into me, laying his big, warm hand possessively on my hip. "Maybe we can go to bed, too. For about an hour or so."

In answer to his tempting proposition, I go up on my tiptoes, clutching him by the back of his neck so that I can kiss him. Mal groans into my mouth, tugging me toward him as he deepens the kiss. I let him, and I nearly decide to say 'screw it' and lead him upstairs, but then I hear high-pitched laughter coming from near the house and, sorry, Mal.

I pull back, moving my hand so that I'm patting his cheek. "Raincheck?"

His brows draw together, the lusty daze in his eyes sharpening at my flippant question.

Huh. Oh. Right.

Rain.

"Sorry. Bad choice of words. I mean, later? I'd like to go outside and see if I can find them for a chat."

"I'd do anything for you, my Shannon—"

Including suffering with a hard-on until it deflates because sex can wait a little bit longer, huh?

I drop my hand, patting the space behind his pecs. I tap the **A** & **N** in my name. "Girl talk, babe. I love Kennedy to death, and most of the villagers are cool, but it's great to talk to any of the girls who still live on Earth. What if Sierra and Hope"—and I gotta know how *that* friendship happened since, last I heard, Billie was Sierra's best friend and her pop persona's manager—"go right back to Earth? To Manhattan or New Jersey or wherever they're living now that's not *here*?"

I need the gossip. The updates. More importantly, how did my TV show end? What movies are coming out? Has any of us figured out how to make the internet work here yet? Magic, turns out, is a great electricity boost. Basic devices like my e-reader and electric shaver get charged by one of Loki's spells, but damn it, I miss my streaming services and my TV!

Get me entertainment like that that works in Sombra and I'll be more than happy to stay for the rest of forever. Until then, I'll stick with the EL, plus getting my fixes when one of the human mates who can still live full-time in the mortal realm—like Hope, Sierra, and Amy—occasionally visit.

Amy is childfree. So is Hope; as she says, she loves her nephew and nieces to pieces, but never wanted any kids of her own. Sierra is about halfway through her pregnancy, only recently starting to show, but since she's probably the most photographed woman in the world, it was definitely a big bombshell that she's giving up her touring life, especially when it was obvious that it was due to settling down and starting a family at the height of her career.

That's right. Whiskey Rose herself, America's pop princess, is mated to a red-eyed Sombra demon hunter named Dagon. She's pregnant with his kid—and I can only imagine the online speculation about who the father must be—and would never have been able to hide it as easily as I did.

Hope, on the other hand, is a sweet if a little scatter-brained librarian from central New Jersey; with her visiting, I'd love to show her the EL and get her opinion on it. The poor girl thought she was being haunted because the *Grimoire du Sombra* was following her around. In reality, since her mage mate, Sammael, was technically a ghost at the time after he tried to cast the matefinder spell himself *and* he was the one trying to get her to read the *verus amor* spell to summon him to her, she *was* being haunted.

I didn't know that, though. When I first met her, Sammael had been taken from her home in the same enchanted gold chains that he once threatened *my* mate with. She drove all the way from Westfield to Jericho to bring the spellbook back to Turn the Page, hoping Kennedy could help. Sorry. She was already living her HEA with Loki, while I was the lucky chick who had to help her save her mate.

So... yeah. Not a big fan of Sammael because, like with Glaine, your girl holds a grudge. Loki's just lucky that I found it in me to forgive him for ramming Mal with his horns, but that's because of Kennedy. I like Hope. If we ever get as close as me and Ken, I might soften toward her mate.

Glaine, though? Billie's awesome, but the grumpy guard hasn't got a prayer.

Malphas likes him. My Mal likes *everyone*.

And that gives me an idea.

"Why don't you go talk to Dagon and Sammael? Keep them company while I go catch up with Hope and Sierra?"

A soft acquiescing sigh from my big demon mate before he says, "Glaine had already found his way over. Loki took Sammael with him, heading off somewhere to talk 'mage', but Glaine was sent to speak with the hunter."

Sent... "Billie made him go?"

I thought I saw their downstairs light on last night. Interesting that the head of Haures's guard was in

Nuit before the rain, but I wouldn't be surprised if he sticks around now *after* it.

Then Haures doesn't have to make an appearance at all, does he?

Malphas nods.

I grin. "Perfect! I'll go wait outside until I see the girls, and you keep Dagon and Glaine company while we have a little girl talk. And," I say, before he can ask, "I'll stay right by the house so I'll know if Alana cries."

One thing I can say about my mate is that he knows when he's beat.

With a nod, he runs the side of his shadow claw against the edge of my jaw. "As you wish, my Shannon."

CHAPTER 8
GIRL TALK

SHANNON

Once I see that Hope, Sierra, and Billie had walked out of Azazel's healer hut, the three of them laughing and chatting, I flag them down.

Sierra waves. So does Hope. Billie, being Billie, just changes her path so that the three of them head over to my house instead of hers and Glaine's.

It's been at least two weeks since Billie's last trip to Nuit. I greet her with as much enthusiasm as I do the other two: by throwing my arms around them each, one after the other.

As soon as we get our greetings out of the way, Hope starts vibrating in place, her obvious excitement ready to spill out before she squeals, "Look, Shannon. It's Whiskey Rose!"

Oh, boy.

I knew that Hope was a huge Whiskey Rose fan. I also knew that Dagon's mate Sierra *is* Whiskey Rose. I already had to listen to Kennedy gush about their first meeting when Sierra and Dagon came to Nuit, looking for Billie after Glaine basically stole her from Sierra's apartment back in Manhattan.

I didn't know that Hope and Sierra were acquainted, but you know what? I'm not surprised. With the exception of Susanna, Duke Haures's mate that he keeps sequestered and hidden in the capital, all the rest of us eventually form bonds due to being a Sombra demon's mate.

Considering Sierra doesn't look annoyed at Hope, I figure one has sprung up between the two.

Instead, Sierra gives her an amused grin. "Hope. I thought we got past this."

"I know." Hope's excited expression turns a touch sheepish. "And, I promise, I'm not like this when we're back home. It's just... I can't believe I'm friends with Whiskey Rose!"

"Yeah. Actually... not gonna lie. I was kind of wondering about that. Did you two come here together, or was it just luck that there are five of us in Nuit together?"

Me. Kennedy. Billie. Sierra. Hope.

There's never been so many of us at one time, and maybe I'm just being suspicious after the rain last night, but... I don't know... it seems kinda omen-ish.

Prophecy-ish.

Hm.

As Billie launches into a quick explanation of how she actually arranged for the two to meet so that they could each rely on the other on Earth while the rest of us were in Sombra, I try to pay attention. It's a good idea, I admit. Glaine, Billie's mate, and Sammael, Hope's mate, had worked together under Duke Haures for centuries. Since Billie decided to stay in the demon world, but Sierra had insisted on sticking it out on Earth a little longer, Sierra might need someone who knew what she was going through.

So Billie had Glaine ask Sammael to find Dagon so that Hope could become friends with Sierra. It obviously worked, even if poor Hope can't shake some of the stars out of her eyes when she remembers that the woman with the gorgeous face, trademark braid, and slight belly bump starred in two movies recently while getting ready for her worldwide music tour.

Hell, I was a little shell-shocked the first time I met Sierra. I'll admit, I've never been all that into pop music. Even when I was younger, I was a total musical theatre kid instead. I knew who Whiskey Rose was, of course. I even knew she'd been in a girl group with two others before they broke up, and she went solo.

Did I recognize that Billie was one of them? Or that the doppelseers' feisty redheaded mate was another?

Nope.

Kennedy did. I bet Hope knows, too. Me? They're just Sierra and Billie… even if there's no better person to ask for the tea than a woman whose face is constantly plastered all over the tabloids.

At Hope's urging—while Billie rolls her eyes—Sierra launches into a story about how the famous playboy… and her infamous ex… Jared Turner found himself in a sticky situation involving a hot tub, a jar of honey, an Olympic skier, and her hockey-playing boyfriend.

She's just winding it down, satisfaction in her voice as she says that he spent the last two months trying to erase his mugshot from the news, when Billie suddenly straightens.

Sierra's former manager/forever best friend hates Jared Turner. Probably not as much as she does *her* ex, who tried to capture Sierra at gunpoint, but it's still a lot. I thought she'd be just as satisfied to hear that Turner was in legal hot water. And maybe she is, but she's also distracted.

"Six," she says, directing it at me.

Huh? "What was that?"

"Just correcting something you said before, Shannon. When you said there were five of us… five human women in Nuit. Not anymore." She jerks her chin over my shoulder. "It's six."

Turning to look behind me, my stomach drops when I see the knock-out with the long, wavy, deep-red hair smiling as she walks toward us. She's flanked by *two* demons. Each one is in his shadow form, a pair of bright purple eyes gleaming out from the inky black depths.

I bite down on my bottom lip nervously.

So, Apollyon wasn't worried about the rain, huh? Sure, he didn't send for Duke Haures or anything, and maybe he didn't contact Lucian and Damien, either—because, you know, *psychics*—but they're here now anyway.

Wonderful.

Even better, I'm not the only one who doesn't seem too thrilled at the appearance of our new guests.

Sierra sucks in a breath, her cheeks hollowing. A soft sigh escapes her as Hope's brow furrows, glancing from Sierra to Tandy and back.

Meanwhile, Billie lays her hand on Sierra's shoulder.

Sierra shakes her head. The universal signal for 'I'm fine, don't worry about it.'

Billie thins her lips and looks down her nose at her best friend. And *that* says 'Bullshit' without her ever having to utter a word.

It hits me a moment later. Oh. *Oh.* I knew about this. It was more ancient gossip, back from the days the three of these women were in their girl group. Like twelve years ago, maybe.

When Sierra actually was *dating* Jared Turner… until he cheated on her with Tandy.

That one act put a schism in their band and their friendship that never healed. Thr33peat split up, Sierra became Whiskey Rose, and the song she wrote about Jared Turner betraying their years-long teenage relationship—*Heart Barely Used*—became her break-out hit.

They hadn't spoken in years. Sierra and Tandy, I mean. At least, not until the doppelseers were searching for their mate about six months ago and they had Malphas draw the woman that they saw in their head.

Tandy Lewis.

Their one true mate—and the woman that Sierra has been avoiding ever since Tandy came to live in Sombra.

Jeez. What does it say about me that I wanted entertainment and, welp, it looks like I might just get it?

Finally. At least *that*'s something to take my mind off of the rain.

MALPHAS

Over the many cycles that we have been bonded, my mate has taught me a lot. Today I'm reminded of the concept of 'female conversations', or as she prefers to call it: girl talk.

It all started with Amy, Nox's human mate. The first time we went to her quarters, Shannon disappeared into another room to speak with her, leaving me and the former Nuit hunter to stand together, waiting for our mates to tire of each other's company and return to their males.

Since then, every time Shannon and I visit the village of Connecticut, the same thing happens. Shannon and Amy talk, and now Nox questions me on what I have learned about being a provider for my mate.

We don't hunt for our mates in the human world, though Nox has made it his purpose to explain to me how. Sometimes he and Amy would even join Shannon and me on our trips to Sombra so that I could put his lessons to use. While baking for my mate makes her happier than bringing her one of the prey beasts that I hunted with Nox, the hunter is right. I must do everything I can to show her how much I love her.

In Jericho, they have something similar to the Sombran ungez. Wee baby cats known as kittens. I don't hunt them, though I help them, and Shannon always beams at me when I rescue another baby cat. Some nights, while we were waiting for Alana to be born, she would tell me she knew she picked the perfect dad for her kid because of the way I treat the kittens. I never would've thought to do anything else, which is probably why I'm the clan artist instead of one of the hunters…

I don't need to be. My mate adores me the way

that I am, and she's not only the perfect mother for my child. She is my heart. My light. My flower. She is tiny, but mighty, and will always be the one to stand before me, defending me and our daughter. She is loving. Smart. Amusing. My love.

And, blunt as ever, she has no issue telling me when she's had enough of my company.

Earlier tonight, as the main moon started to shine through the shadows in the sky, Shannon put Alana down for a nap after dinner, then shooed me outside, sending me to the village square. With Sierra and Hope staying over another night—and the doppelseers hesitant to return to their enchanted house with their mate—the six human women decided to gather in front of our house for another round of 'girl talk'.

It's a lovely night. The heat warms you down to your shadows, and though it's been days since the gold moon rose, the main moon is shining brightly, cutting through some of the usual gloom. The women are either sitting on our porch or milling around out front as they chat, with my mate positioned near the slightly open window in case Alana coos and calls for her mother.

I said my hellos to Sammael, Dagon, Lucian, and Damien earlier. I waited to see if the doppelseers would mention the fleeting rainfall from last night, or even tell us if there had been a change to the prophecy involving Alana, but instead, the other males all act as though there's nothing to fret about, even though they acknowledge that it did happen—and it's part of the reason they've stopped in to visit Nuit.

The other? A riddle from Damien that this is where their mate is meant to be. Since she easily joined in on the 'girl talk'—while notably avoiding Dagon's fair-haired mate—the doppelseer must be right, though I can't stop remembering the sting of the raindrops falling against my skin.

I am the only one. It seems as though everyone I spoke to seemed to be in a fine, worry-free mood. In fact, Apollyon welcomed the doppelseers' sudden visit by deciding a village feast was in order. With Loki and Kennedy's spawn almost here, and Azazel confirming that Dagon and Sierra's spawn is doing well, the clan leader and clanmother had the feast planned and hosted for dinner tonight to celebrate our growing clan, plus our honor in hosting the doppelseers and their mate.

And if the sense of camaraderie has anything to do with my mentioning to Apollyon earlier this morning that I can no longer stand to see some of my fellow demons treating Shannon and Alana with anything less than a friendly graciousness, otherwise we might have to relocate to a village that *will*, I'm sure that's all just a coincidence…

Lilith is fond of my family. Apollyon listens to Lilith, and if Duke Haures learned that any of his subjects were wary of my daughter because she was born like him… born without shadows and with pale, colorless skin… then I'm sure he might find it in him to visit Nuit again.

And I doubt anyone wants *that*.

After the feast, the females decided to return to their earlier conversation. Loki went off to talk with Apollyon and Sammael; the two mages said they weren't concerned with the report of rain that I gave to Apollyon earlier this morning, but between them and the clan leader, they wanted to discuss what it might've meant—and how to stop it from happening inside of Nuit again.

Lucian and Damien disappeared, too. Since they left Tandy behind in the care of Sierra and Billie, I know they haven't used their enchanted house to relocate to another part of Sombra. Instead, the doppelseers are probably doing things that only another clan seer might understand. And since Caldor, our last seer—and the one who told me I'd find my forever with a mate that blooms in a sun that never shines in Sombra, something I never understood until my Shannon summoned me to her—had moved to Soleil to stay with the one true mate he finally divined for himself, we don't have one.

Sometimes, I wish I could see. That, instead of using giz and paint to draw the images in my mind's eye, I saw something that would help keep my family safe.

It's not to be. Instead, I worry about a future I can not fight, though if the gods are merciful, maybe I can change it…

The rain has changed everything; that, plus how I upset my mate. I tried to protect her, to shield her, the way a gentle Sombra demon could, but I was wrong. I messed up. I should've known better, and my shame is hard to hide as I stand with Dagon and Glaine, the other two banished from our mates' 'girl talk' session.

The duke's head guard splits his time between Mavro, where he still serves Duke Haures, and Nuit, where he helps Apollyon keep Nuit safe. With Billie's kin come to visit with her, Glaine has also extended his stay in town. That doesn't mean he hasn't sent his own message to Duke Haures about the inexplicable, sudden rain. He told me earlier that he had; so did Apollyon, with Loki's help. But since the duke has stayed in the capital with his mate, Glaine and Dagon both agree that he doesn't think that the prophecy is unfolding just yet.

He's not concerned. I try not to be. And maybe if I wasn't worrying so much, I would've noticed much sooner that something… something was wrong.

At first, I think it's just me. I went more than a thousand years without mating. The most I did was rub my cock to the promise of the female meant for me, but even that lost any enjoyment over the centuries. Tasting Shannon's cunt… feeling the way she wraps around my length tightly whenever she invites me into her body… the first time we mated, I knew that that was what I had spent the last millennium waiting for. Her affection, her love, her trust as I penetrated her, and the pleasure that consumed me when I found my one true mate.

I will never tire of pleasuring my female. Even now, my mouth waters to lap at her cunt. My cock is so hard, I add another layer of shadows to my coverings to hide how desperate I am for her all of a sudden. Usually I can control myself much better than this. I will always want my Shannon, but I've never felt as though I'd claw through my own skin to get inside of hers.

I grit my teeth. Folding my fingers, I jab my claws into the flesh of my solid palm. A trickle of blood stains my skin from where I accidentally nick it. Transforming my hands to shadow and back, my hands a hazy black to their usual red, I heal the injury.

Neither Dagon nor Glaine notice.

Odd.

CHAPTER 9
NEED

MALPHAS

It hits me that both demons are quiet. So am I. Sweat slicks my brow. Sombra is a fiery world, of ash and shadows. Our coolest days are ones that Shannon would never leave the apartment, preferring to park herself in front of the cold air vent—the AC—in our human home. It took her a while to get used to the dry yet oppressive heat in Sombra, but, to me, it's *my* home. It doesn't bother me.

So why am I feeling feverish?

And that's not all. My cock aches. My sac is tight. I am in my demon form, but my skin almost itches. It's sensitive without my shadows being out, and even my horns beg to be stroked. I lock my knees to keep them from going even weaker.

My tongue darts out, dabbing the corner of my

suddenly dry mouth. I swipe my brow with the back of my hand.

Still, Glaine and Dagon are too distracted to sense my discomfort.

The soldier has shifted his body. Instead of facing Dagon and me, he's moved so that he can watch the females, his green eyes drawn unblinkingly to the one with wild, gold-colored curls. Billie. She's laughing as she pokes the braided female next to her. Sierra, Dagon's mate

Like all Sombra demons, Dagon is possessive of his mate. Since he and Sierra created their own spawn during a recent gold moon, the hunter is even more so. And yet… Dagon isn't watching his mate as closely as Glaine is.

Instead, he's watching the *sky*.

I follow his stare, and that's when I notice *what* he's staring at.

There is a second moon, an *unusual* one. Not as large as the one that appears every night in Sombra, but bigger still than the gold moon that only rises once every cycle. It's hidden behind one of the dark ash clouds—a mixture of smoke and haze that the ash fields give off—but I see part of the outline peeking through.

I don't know why it has caught his attention. Especially when, just as I think I'm the only male feeling this sudden need for his mate, Dagon rips his head away from the sky, hand going to his crotch as he grumbles softly under his breath.

"Dagon?" The bold way he palms his cock through his leathers distracts me for a moment from how much mine longs for Shannon. "Are you alright?"

"It's the mate sickness," he grates. "I thought that I would never have to feel it again once I completed the essence exchange with Sierra. We are bonded. She is going to have our spawn. There's no reason the sickness should have returned."

Is that what I'm feeling?

I think about how eager I am to lay Shannon down on our bedding and bury my face in her cunt until I've passed out, her taste the only thing on my lips.

Then I remember how ill she was after I initiated the essence exchange, but before we were bonded. Because I had Shannon's essence—not my finest moment, I admit, since I basically took it from her as she had no idea she was even offering it—she was the one who the gods gave the mate sickness to. It was to urge her to recognize me as her one true mate. The only cure? An intimate touch that led to my mate allowing me to kiss her cunt for the first time.

I never experienced the mate sickness. I always knew that she was meant to be mine, so the gods granted it to Shannon instead.

But if Dagon *has* experienced it…

"Is that what this is?" I ask, not sure what's worse: the sudden horror I feel, or the lust.

Shannon experienced this? Because of me? I should be cursed with a cockstand that will never deflate for ever making my mate suffer such wild, painful *want*.

Dagon nods. "Yes. I remember it well. It's worse, though, because I can sense it creeping down my bond toward Sierra. If she doesn't feel the need now, she will soon."

And so will Shannon.

I tap my fang with my tongue. My mouth is getting drier. My knees buckle again as though they're propelling me to go toward my mate.

I brace my feet in the ash. No. Shannon has never shied away from accepting me. However, she rarely gets to do 'girl talk' with Sierra and Hope. They don't often visit Sombra—Hope and Sammael living permanently on Earth, and Sierra and Dagon only coming to check in with the healer—and it would be very selfish of me to interrupt her because I want to mate her.

So I stay with Dagon and Glaine even if my eyes keep slipping over to where Shannon is leaning comfortably against the house, legs crossed, arms folded behind her head, hair spread out behind her similar to the way it falls against our pillow when I have her under me…

A rough swallow, a stifled moon, and then a short

gasp as, out of the shadows further down the village square, Lucian and Damien come stalking back into Nuit.

Damien, the quiet, more intense twin, veers right for the females. He doesn't stop until he reaches his fire-haired mate, Tandy. Scooping her up easily, settling her over his shoulder, her throaty laugh cuts through the sudden silence as he whisks her away.

Lucian, meanwhile, heads right for us.

His arrival finally catches Glaine's attention. The guard's head swivels while Dagon frowns.

Lucian points up. "For ages, all I've seen is red," he intones. "And now so do we all."

I follow his point. The ash clouds have slipped away, leaving the second moon fully on display.

Before, when I caught Dagon peering up at it, I couldn't understand why. Now that I see the deep blood-red moon shining out of the sky, I'm in awe of it. It's striking. Beautiful. *Terrifying.* My first instinct is to return to my home, grab my paints and my brushes, and come as close to capturing it as I can on canvas.

I've never seen anything like it.

"What is that?" Glaine demands. "That's not the gold moon."

It can't be.

Lucian agrees. "It is the fabled red moon." *Fabled...* "The last time I actually saw one, it was on the night that Queen Alana and King Yelios finalized their mate bond."

So distracted by the unfamiliar mate sickness, I didn't really understand what I was seeing until Lucian confirmed it's a red moon and mentioned Sombra's former rulers. I wasn't wrong when I said that I've never seen anything like it. I haven't, but that's because the last time it shined down on Sombra, I didn't exist yet.

The story of Queen Alana and her mate is a tragedy in Sombran lore. She was a beloved demoness queen—the strongest and best of us all—and the namesake for my Alana. She ruled Sombra for centuries before finding her one true mate: a young soldier named Yelios. She invited him to share her throne, then bonded to him before she elevated him to head of her guard, allowing him to lead her campaign to ward off Sombra's enemies.

King Yelios had one moon with Queen Alana— the *red* moon—before she was martyred in a skirmish when Cindralis tried to invade Sombra more than twenty-five hundred years ago. As our ruler, she insisted on joining the charge of soldiers, and though she pushed back the fire demons, her death was the one my people felt the hardest.

Of course, no one felt it harder than the king, who blamed our enemies that he survived while his mate perished. For the next five centuries, he stood before the throne alone, waging wars with any demon realm who opened their portals to him and his soldiers. To make up for Queen Alana's death, he made moves to colonize them, to bring them under his rule.

Until two thousand years ago—and more than a millennium before I was born—when Haures rose up against Yelios, ousting him from the crystal throne, before disappearing the old king forever.

Stories say he walked into the shadows, choosing to end his existence so that he could finally be reunited with his beloved mate. No one has ever heard from or seen the imposing green-eyed soldier-turned-king since then, and I only think of Yelios now because Lucian mentioned him, and because of the red moon shining ominously over my head.

I understand the mate sickness now. When Sombra's ruler takes their mate, the world celebrates with them. The red moon brings all mated pairs together, their mating a blessing that represents an eternity of well-wishes for our liege.

It's a story. Like Lucian said, a fable.

But as I palm my erection again, I'm not so sure about that anymore.

Glaine glares up at the moon while Dagon regards it warily. "Why is it out now?"

"I don't know," admits the doppelseer. "Haures is a bondmaster. For his own reasons, he's held the red moon back after he bonded Susanna to him."

"Because he's kept her hidden," suggests Glaine. "Very few Sombrans even know she exists."

I do because of the name written in the *Grimoire du Sombra*, and because Susanna Benoit is Amy's kin. Dagon was a hunter-turned-chosen guard for the duchess. Glaine, of course, is the head of Duke Haures's guard.

And Lucian knows nearly *everything*.

His nod says that Glaine has a point. "Yes, but maybe this is his way of sharing his mate with the rest of Sombra."

"His Grace will never do that," cuts in Dagon. "He loves Susanna too much. He won't even let her out of the garden if he has the choice. Until Sombra is safe... no. He wouldn't willingly share her now."

Maybe not, but there's no denying the red moon is out, and I'm in desperate need of my mate.

Glaine doesn't argue with Dagon. Instead, his gaze going back to Billie, he asks, "Is the red moon the same as the gold moon in other ways?"

Ah. I understand. My Shannon... she doesn't want any other spawn. As she said, with Alana, she is 'one and done'. If I fully mate her while the red moon is out, will she conceive?

"No," says Lucian, to my relief—and to Glaine's, too. He and his mate have chosen to be like Amy and Nox: no spawn for them for now. "It is all about the pleasure. Of enjoying your mate until the red moon sets come morning as we reinforce our bonds just as the duke and his mate must be." His purple eyes flicker, and he glances over his shoulder in time to see

Damien disappearing out of Nuit with Tandy. "Just like my twin and I shall enjoy ours."

With one last nod, Lucian turns, striding after his brother and their mate.

Glaine doesn't hesitate, either. His jaw set, he starts toward the females, his intent to break up the 'girl talk' obvious. Then again, Billie's head turns, meeting the hunger in his expression as he strides over. She murmurs something to Sierra, then starts jogging toward her mate, breaking it up herself.

Dagon claps me on the shoulder. "Just a touch will help with the mate sickness," he says, "but if the red moon insists we pleasure our females… isn't that what an honorable male would do?"

He follows behind Glaine.

I forget all about my fellow demons as I search for my Shannon.

Our eyes meet.

Dull yet pretty, her deep blue gaze seems to glimmer and gleam in invitation as she rises from her lean. And I know—because I know my mate—that the red moon *is* affecting her. That, or she simply knows her male, and will always, always welcome him when he needs her.

And because I *am* her male, I will give her what *she* needs.

The females have scattered by the time I reach her. Glaine has taken Billie. Dagon has Sierra. Tandy has slipped out into the eve with her mates. Loki and

Sammael haven't returned yet, but Kennedy sidles back to her home, taking Hope with her.

And then there's Shannon.

She raises the furry strips of pale hair over her lust-filled eyes.

Without any warning, I heft my mate up in my arms, tilting Shannon so that one hand cradles her back, the other tucked securely beneath her knees. Her squeal of delight jumps right to my cock.

And I know that, whatever happens tonight, it'll be a night to remember.

SHANNON

Sierra waves one hand in front of her face, the other cradling her small baby bump. "God-damn, I thought New York in summer was hellish. This? This is actual hell."

Tandy makes a small sound of agreement. Sierra completely pretends that she didn't hear it.

Half of me wants to tell them to cut the shit and just figure it out. Considering Billie already has and has decided to stop acting like an intermediary so that they do, I feel like it would be better if I keep my trap shut.

Besides, their decade-long beef is between them. Tandy wants Sierra's forgiveness while Sierra insists that there's nothing to forgive which is, well, horseshit, basically. Tandy fucked her man behind her back. I'd hold a grudge over that, too.

Luckily, this is the first time they've been in the village together. Unluckily, the obvious rift between them got old when we were chatting earlier. I'd figured that, after the feast, either Tandy would leave with her twin mates or Sierra and Hope would announce that they were heading back with Dagon and Sammael. No way would they want to torture us all again with this awkward small talk.

Nope. Tandy mentioned that Damien and Lucian were here because they saw they were supposed to be here so they weren't leaving anytime soon. As for Sierra and Hope, they might've wanted to go except Sammael and Loki took off for 'mage' business after dinner. The foursome came together and planned on leaving together, so with Sammael missing, they were also sticking around.

Kennedy had been resting earlier during our first chat. She's with us now, trying her best to hide how excited she is to be hanging out with the members of Thr33peat while I excuse myself to check on Alana.

Now my baby is fed, changed, and sleeping for the night. I'm still parked in front of the window in case she wakes up and I hear her moving around, but staying outside of the house while she's sleeping inside is perfectly safe in a village like Nuit.

Hell, we don't even lock our doors and windows here…

It is hot, though. Every time I think that I've gotten used to it, it's like some higher beings—the Sombran gods, maybe—decide to crank it up another degree or two.

For some reason, it's even worse tonight. I'm thirty-two in a twenty-nine-year-old's body. No way should I be having hot flashes, but ever since I slipped outside again to join in with the girl talk, it's like I'm on fire.

Hope is talking now, with Kennedy nodding eagerly, but I'm barely listening. Then again, she's kinda not talking anymore, either. Her voice trails off as she looks behind her, as if searching for something.

Or someone?

Me? I'd be lying if I wasn't distracted by staring at Malphas. Unnf. It forever turns me on that his outfit of choice is a pair of leathers—or shadows—that cover up the cock that belongs to me and me alone, and then nothing else. From the moment he had my name tattooed on his chest with silver ink, he shows it off every chance he can. His hair is long, thick, and luscious. His features masculine and strong, and I've got a certain weakness for his horns.

Nothing like a built-in handlebar when I want to ride his face, am I right?

He has his back to me, standing over there with Glaine and Dagon while I don't bother hiding the fact that I'm ogling his ass.

I do feel a tiny twinge of guilt for sending him out

there earlier, like a mom shipping her kid off to a playdate with the neighborhood boys. He must've enjoyed himself since, like the human women, he returned to talk to them after dinner. I almost wish I could hear what they're saying, but since Dagon is staring off into space and Glaine is staring over here at Billie, my mate's probably as bored as I am.

No. Not bored.

Horny.

That's what this anxious, distracting feeling is. Shit. I try to discreetly rub my thighs together, giving my throbbing pussy a little relief, all while mentally undressing my mate from across the square. Damn. The curve of his ass and just how tight it is… he has me licking my lips in desire.

I remember how there were stages in my early pregnancy where I honestly thought I would die if Malphas didn't fuck me. This? I don't know where it came from, as sudden as this need is, but *shit*. It's, like, ten times worse.

Hm. Would cutting the others off mid-sentence and saying, "Sorry, need some shadow dick," be too much? Probably. If it was just Amy standing here, I would. Kennedy? Definitely. If Lilith had joined us, she would laugh; she thinks I'm an amusing human who talks too much, and she isn't wrong at all. I've gotten to know Billie enough to consider her a friend, but this relationship with Sierra and Hope is too new to blow them off to get my back blown out.

Same with Tandy—

Whoa. Hold on. I blink, then do a double-take. A second ago, Tandy was standing right there, twirling a strand of vibrant red hair around her pointer finger, trying her best not to look as awkward as she obviously feels. I didn't even see him coming, but one of the doppelseers—hell if I know which—just scooped her up, tossing her over his shoulder before striding away from the rest of us.

Their path is taking them out of Nuit. Makes sense. The psychic twins own this enchanted cabin that reminds me of Howl's Moving Castle. It drifts all over Sombra, going where they're needed. They would've parked it just outside of Nuit's borders, and that's where he's taking her now.

"Guess we're not the only ones feeling hot," remarks Billie. "Would be nice if Glaine remembered I existed, but nope. Look. They're all staring up at the sky."

My head swivels back over to the guys. The other twin is there with them, talking to Malphas, Glaine, and Dagon, and Billie's right. They're watching the moon—

No. *Moons.*

Weird. The gold moon just came and went, and I've never seen any other one apart from the regular moon… until now. I wonder what that's about?

Just as I have that thought, Malphas tugs on our bond. It might be on purpose, it might've been on accident, but I get the sensation that he needs me, too. A second later, I burst out laughing. After being bonded mates for as long as we have, it's easy to dip into his essence. I don't often do it, but you know what they say. Curiosity kills the cat.

Or, in this case, goes straight to my poor pussy.

Because the new moon? The red moon?

It's a *mating* moon.

"They're looking up at a horny moon, Bil."

She raises her eyebrows. "What was that, Shannon?"

Please. "Oh, come on. You feel it." I wiggle my fingers back at the guys. "My mate *really* feels it. I was trying to pretend like I didn't, but one of Tandy's mates just told Mal about the red moon up there. See it? Seems like it's responsible for it."

Billie sighs, her big baby blues glittering in amusement regardless. "Just when I'm getting used to living here."

"You complaining?"

"When Glaine is my mate? You must be joking." She laughs, and Sierra bumps her shoulder playfully. "In fact, speak of the demon…"

Glaine's peeled off from the group. He's stalking over to ours, a look of absolute purpose on his face. Grabbing her hand, he starts guiding her back to their place.

As she goes, she calls out, "We'll be heading upstairs. I still have a couch if you need it, Sierra.

Hope, have your mage whip up a spare if you need it, or maybe bunk with Kennedy and Loki. See you on the other side, ladies."

While Hope, Sierra, and Kennedy exchange an amused look, I turn back in time to see that Mal and Dagon have broken up the last of their circle. Sensing how much he needs me, I shouldn't have been surprised that Mal stalks right over to me, lifting me easily, tilting me back into a bridal-style carry.

And, to be fair, I'm not. Not really. I do squeal in anticipation as he lifts me, and I only hope that, when I see the other girls for girl talk later, they've had as enjoyable of a night as I'm about to.

***

THERE'S NO DEBATING IT. RED MOON OR NOT, WE need to fuck. We need to mate. I want Mal, he's desperate for me, and I don't see any reason why we shouldn't give in to our love and desire for each other.

But we're, you know, responsible parents; at least, we try our best to be. Once I kick my legs a little, signaling for Mal to put me down, I gesture to the stairs. "Let me make sure Alana is sleeping. Stay down here."

Mal cocks his head, showing off his slick, beautiful horns. "You don't want to mate in our room?"

"Maybe later, babe. If this red moon thing is as potent as I think, it might be too close to Alana's room. I'm figuring this might be an all-night thing, right?"

His tongue darts out, dabbing the point of his fang. "Hopefully."

That's what I thought. "We can't go too far. The lava pool is out of the question since Kennedy's gonna be too busy to babysit for us. That means we let Alana sleep in her crib upstairs, and we can have our fun down here on the couch. Sound good?"

He bows his head, taking a quick kiss. "You want me to check on her?"

"I'll go. You get ready for me."

That won't be difficult. He has his leathers on, and that's all. But since I like to tease my mate a little, make him hungry for me, I blow him a kiss, then disappear up the stairs.

Just like I thought, Alana is fast asleep. I ruffle her curls, swipe her cheek with my thumb, then tell her a sweet good night before returning to Mal.

He's sitting on the couch, completely bare. His erection is jutting out from the juncture of his legs. It's big and it's daunting, the blood rushing to it turning the red skin nearly purple, and if I didn't know I could fit that sucker inside of me, I'd be wary.

"Come here, my flower," he rumbles, reaching out for me with his shadow claws as he spreads his legs, leaving me a gap to approach him.

I hold up my finger.

"We have to be quiet," I tell him. "I don't want to wake her up."

"Anything for you, my mate."

I grab the hem of my tank top, lifting it up and over my head before tossing it to the floor. My bra goes next. "I mean it, Mal. I need you. Fuck it, I *crave* you. Red moon or not, if I don't have your hands on me… your mouth on me… I might die."

Mal's golden eyes glitter with lust and amusement as he zeroes in on my full tits. "You are immortal."

I unbutton my jeans, tug on the zipper, and start shimmying them off. "I can still *feel* like I'm dying."

"Then you have no need to worry." He lifts his big hands, flexing his fingers again. "Come here and let your male touch you."

I wait until I'm completely naked before I do. Sidling over to him, I step between his legs, bracing myself on his broad shoulders. His skin is hot; I'm sure mine is, too. The red moon is doing a number on us, and I *love* it.

Mal reaches out, his palms scalding my skin as he takes a tit in each of his hands. I throw back my head, moaning at how pleasurable it feels to have his shadow claws dipping past my skin, his fingertips kneading at my tender flesh.

I thread my fingers through his thick hair as he plays with my tits, worshipping them, loving them. He squeezes. Flicks. Strokes.

It feels *amazing*.

I need more, though, and I throw my leg over his thigh, climbing onto his lap while he fondles me. He jolts when my wet pussy touches his skin, his touch getting a little firmer and a whole lot more possessive.

"Shannon," he hisses.

"Good boy," I murmur because, if there's one thing I learned about Mal, he likes it when I praise him, especially during sex. "You're keeping your voice down, just like I asked."

"Your cunt… it feels so good on my skin."

"Well, back atcha, babe. Your hands are magic on my tits. But don't forget about the rest of me. Your mate is a needy girl tonight."

As if remembering that he can touch my pussy, too, if he wants—he can do a whole lot to it—he releases my breasts, pausing only when he sees what he's done.

"Milk?" he marvels.

Hey. I'm not embarrassed. This man sticks his tongue in my pussy on a regular basis. Once, he missed, and I found out what it was like to have my ass eaten. Of course, that led to us exploring other avenues of pleasure… but in the last four months, Mal has—consciously or not—avoided playing with my tits as if he's decided they belong to our daughter while I'm nursing.

He was fondling them, playing with them, swiping over my nips with his shadow claws… is it any surprise that I leaked a little?

"I'm always ready in case Alana's hungry."

"Our spawn might not be, but your male… he is starved for you."

Mal ducks his head just enough to bring his mouth down to my tit. He doesn't suckle, though he does lap at my nipple, taking enough of the breast milk inside of him that my body shivers.

"Oh, baby," I breathe out, squirming to get closer to his heat. "I love it when I get to see your kinky side."

"It's you." His voice is both raspy and solemn as he pulls away from my tit, looking up at my face in earnestness instead. "Every part of you is delicious, my mate. I could feast on you for eternity and never hunger. Your cunt… your milk. Whatever you offer, I will gladly accept."

"No. I want you to *take* it."

He groans.

I squeeze his thigh, slipping a little in the mess I'm making on him. "Is that quiet, Mal?"

"My apologies. But… oh, my mate… you don't know what the idea of doing that… of just taking you… of making you mine… I am an honorable male—"

"Sure are."

"—but I admit that I fantasize of flipping you to your belly, mounting you, and mating you while you squirm in pleasure beneath me."

Well, *fuck*. Now that Mal's put that in my head, I'm also fantasizing about it.

When I was pregnant nearly our entire relationship so far, Mal's been careful with me when it comes to mating. Plus, you know, there's our size difference to think of. No denying he's huge and, being proportionate, that means his dick is pretty freaking huge, too.

But I can take him. I'm four months postpartum, my body has figured out that Mal's only gives pleasure, and I have learned all the way down to the depths of my soul that this demon will never, ever hurt me.

I lick my lips and grin up at Mal. "Then do it."

His brow furrows. "Do you… does my mate request it?"

Oh, Malphas. Even now, he needs permission.

I lift my hand, cradling his sharp jaw. "Hell, yeah, she requests it."

That's all he needs to let himself go.

Hooking his hands under my arms, Mal lifts me easily. I'm up, legs dangling, squealing again as he shifts me with care before laying me down on my belly on the couch. I scoot just enough so that I can grip the arm of it before stretching out, wiggling my toes as Mal climbs on top of me.

He's in his demon form. At this point, we've fucked in every single one of his shapes and sizes, but there's something about a seven-foot demon with superheated skin using his big body to pleasure mine.

He's always careful. No matter what, he keeps his claws shadow so that he doesn't accidentally jab me, and I know that he'll turn his dick to shadow if only because it heightens both of our pleasure when he does.

There's no resistance, either. When he can make his dick the right size for me so that it's not too narrow, not too tight, and that he can bottom out without making me feel so stuffed that I'm gonna ache, why wouldn't he?

He doesn't put his full weight on me. Bracing himself, he still manages to cage me in, pinning me down as he positions himself at the entrance to my pussy.

One thrust is all it takes for him to seat himself inside of me, both of us moaning now at just how perfect it feels to be connected tonight of all nights.

On our way inside, he assured me we could mate all night without worrying about getting pregnant again; this is a rare red moon, after all, not the gold one. And that is the only reason why, when he starts panting my name, quickening his pace, coming within a minute or two of first starting to fuck me, I'm not mad.

Besides, he'll be ready to go in seconds. As for me, the sensation of having me under him, plus knowing he wants me so desperately even aware that he can't last, has me orgasming along with him.

Or, you know, maybe it's the red moon.

It's probably the red moon.

God bless the red moon…

Finally, coming down from my climax, I have to admit that, damn it, we weren't quiet at all—and that's because, sorry, I'm a screamer, and I can't help it. Knowing that was just the first round of what promises to be many, I doubt we'll be quiet then, either. Thankfully, Alana has proven that she can sleep through the night whenever I need my mate, so maybe she will.

If not, I'll hear her, and I'll go to her. But, until then, I'm going to enjoy my mate for as long as the red moon lasts—and after that, too.

SHANNON

Something's wrong.

You'd think that after the banging of a lifetime that Malphas gave me, I'd be boneless and relaxed. Barring that, I'd be oversensitized and tender. I think he ended up making me come no less than ten times, and I'm pretty sure I finally fell asleep with his dick in my mouth like a pacifier.

Physically, I feel fine. Better than fine. Malphas told me that the red moon is a rare event where the mated couples in Sombra can't resist the urge to mate and re-finalize their bond. I don't know what it was like for the *un*mated demons last night, but for their sakes—because I know how loud *I* can get—I hope they went to bed and put their pillows over their heads. If the consuming lust hit them, too, and they had to masturbate alone all night… yeah. That would've sucked.

I like to think that wasn't the case. I mean, Alana slept through it just fine.

Right?

I… I don't know. My girl always sleeps peacefully through the night, but with the red moon doing a number on us, she might've decided she needed a midnight snack and, downstairs on the couch, I might not have heard her.

I have no idea what time it is. In a shadow realm, it's hard to guess, so I kinda just go with the rhythm of my body's clock. It's telling me that I slept in later than I usually do. My breasts feel heavy, both from the way Mal fondled them last night and because it might be past time for Alana's breakfast.

We're still in the living room, where we finally fell asleep. It's so rare that I'm up and he isn't that, for a few contented seconds, I just watch his chest rise and fall. He's solid, taking up most of the couch. I did wake up with my head in his lap, my feet tucked under his cheek, but even as he sprawled out on his back, he was careful to keep me as comfortable as possible.

I grin and, padding softly in bare feet, I move toward the window.

It has to be morning. Between how long the red moon had us mating, then how deeply I fell asleep when we were done, it's been hours. Just to make sure, though, I want to peek outside and check that the red moon has set.

I look—and my heart nearly fucking stops.

The red moon is gone. Good. Great. There's no way I'd miss the blood-red orb hanging high in the sky.

Just like I don't miss the steady rain falling over Sombra.

Rain.

It's raining.

Again.

Alana…

The last time it rained, my baby was crying. It stopped as soon as she did, and as I run toward the stairs, my heart thumping as wildly as it hopes, I tell myself there's nothing wrong. I'm just being paranoid. Maybe she's upset because her parents slept downstairs. Maybe she's hungry.

Or maybe she's gone.

Because Alana… she's *gone.* Her window is closed. The crib is empty. All that's left is her rumpled bedding.

My baby is *missing.*

When I finally realize what exactly that means, I scream so loudly, there's a good chance I don't just wake up my mate.

I think I wake up the entire *village.*

THERE IS NO ONE IN THIS WORLD OR ANY OTHER THAT could've brought me back from the brink of collapse except for Malphas.

My mate came flying into the room almost as soon as I started to scream. He took one look at the empty crib while I sobbed and gasped and babbled Alana's name, then quickly started conjuring his shadows. Bottom coverings for him, plus something that hits me from chest to ass because he must've known that, as soon as I got the despair out of my system, it would immediately turn to rage.

He's right. As though my consciousness was just waiting for me not to be naked and vulnerable, once we were covered, I was on the move. Though Alana is advanced, she's not *so* advanced that she can leave her crib and crawl around the two levels of our home. Still, I checked every room. Mal was right there as I did, double-checking the nooks and crannies I couldn't reach. We both know that—for the moment —Alana doesn't have any shadows. She can't turn to mist or go black and transparent, but Malphas searched as though she's a full demon child just in case.

But he doesn't find her. Neither do I.

As soon as we considered the house clear, I ran out into the rain. It's warm, but I can deal, even though most of the villagers linger on their porches versus coming down to be nosy where I can see them.

I was right. My scream woke up *everyone*, though

maybe the rain had something to do with that. Screw a five-minute storm. This is the real thing, and if I've already thought that Alana's disappearance might have something to do with the prophecy, I push that thought out of my head.

Fuck the prophecy. I just want my baby back home where she belongs.

Apollyon is one of the other Sombra demons willing to brave the rain *and* my pain. Normally, I'd be grateful that Lilith is right by his side, murmuring soft reassurances, but I don't want to hear them right now. Telling me that everything will be fine, that we'll find Alana, and the rain will stop… it's so hard when the rage buckles under the weight of panic.

I cling to Malphas. He runs his fingers through my damp hair, and if the rain stings like it did two nights ago, he doesn't react like the droplets do. Instead, all I can sense is his helplessness creeping down our bond; it echoes mine.

Still, when he murmurs, "We *will* find her, my Shannon," I hear the promise. I hear the vow.

I want to believe *him*.

It's Malphas. My true love. The father of my missing child. The talented artist who designed Alana's painted nursery…

She'll return to it. I'll do everything I can to make sure of it.

This is my fault. I'm her mother. I don't care how much the call of the red moon pulled me toward

Malphas, that's no excuse. Somehow… somehow my daughter went *missing*, and I can't explain it.

That makes it so, so much worse.

Luckily, Apollyon is thinking rationally. While he and Lilith try their best as leaders of Nuit to keep Mal and me calm, he also engaged help from some of the other villagers—and the visitors who ended up staying overnight due to the red moon.

Thank fucking god. Dagon and Sierra are still here, and of all the hunters in Nuit, Dagon is supposed to be one of the best at tracking.

On Apollyon's orders, he's looking for some sign that Alana left the house. Either because he can scent her or… or if someone took her—

Who would've taken my baby?

Damn it!

"It's all because of the red moon!" I burst out, shoving away from my mate.

I would never blame Mal, not when all of that blame belongs to me, but I need to do something. Since I can't just run off into the night when I don't even know for sure that Alana is out here somewhere, I'm sticking close to the house in case I hear her coo. Considering I can't hear shit over the thud of my heart, I doubt I will, and that just makes me *angrier.*

The golden-eyed clan leader nods slowly. "Perhaps. The red moon definitely… affected most of Nuit last night. Probably all of Sombra."

Perhaps.

Probably.

I'm angry. I'm ashamed. I'm *scared.*

But, deep down, I'm also Shannon Crewes. So, instead of listening to Apollyon's wishy-washy response, I turn to look at his mate. "You get shadow dicked down, Lilith? Was it so irresistible you'd somehow lose your own child? Or am I just a shitty mom?"

Apollyon's mouth falls open, visibly scandalized. Mal moves forward tentatively, his solid hand brushing against mine, letting me know he's right there for me when I need him.

Lilith, though, just keeps a small, reassuring smile on her pretty face. "I've experienced countless gold moons since I came to live with Apollyon as his mate. The red moon was something else entirely."

I should've expected an answer like that. Unlike some of the other villagers, the clan mother has always been fond of me. Since starting the EL, we've become close. Normally, I wouldn't mouth off to Mal's clan leader in case he booted us out of Nuit, but desperate times call for desperate measures.

In between fighting the urge to hide my head under a blanket so I can pretend this isn't a living nightmare and taking off to feel like I'm doing anything to search for Alana, I give Apollyon a 'so there' look.

The red moon… I try to remember what Malphas told me about it. Granted, I was so damn horny, I was barely paying attention as I began to strip off my clothes and get my hands on Mal's dick, but there's something…

My back goes ramrod straight. "Did Haures do this?" I ask. My voice is soft, almost as though I know I shouldn't voice my suspicions, but I can't help it. "He's been super weird about Alana since she was born. If it's a ruler thing, and he's also a bondmaster… did he…"

Did he find a way to summon the red moon to use as a distraction to take our baby?

Because of the damn prophecy?

I don't finish asking my question. Not out loud, at least. I don't have to.

"You cannot blame his Grace—"

"No," I cut in. "You're right. It's *my* fault."

"Shannon—"

I shake my head. "I shouldn't have let it happen, Mal."

"What?" he asks, and his voice is nearly drowned out by the steady fall of rain. "What did you do wrong, my mate? What could you have done differently? You insisted we check on her first. That we mated on the first floor so we didn't disturb her. You did everything right… but if you think you are to blame, so am I."

Blame Mal? I… I can't do that.

Which means I go right back to my top suspect.

"It had to have been the duke," I spit out,

knowing that just saying that could earn me a stint in his dungeons while wearing enchanted chains. I don't care. Deep down, I can't shake the sensation that Haures has something to do with Alana's inexplicable disappearance.

"It wasn't."

At the certainty in the male's voice coming from behind me, I whirl around.

It's Dagon, and his expression tells me two things: that he isn't just standing up for the demon duke out of some innate sense of loyalty, and that he found something that backs up his certainty.

"How do you know?"

"Because I found prints," is his answer. "Boot prints. Human boot prints." He pauses, then drops the bomb on me:

"Human *male* boot prints."

CHAPTER 12
VOW

MALPHAS

No matter how many years I live in Nuit, I will never get used to the skulls that line the edge of Sombra's shadows just outside of our village.

A near-impenetrable wall of darkness, not even the hunters walk too far inside of them. To hunt the prey beasts that feed our village, they don't have to. Only the predators—like the arkoda or the cambroga —live further inside. Same as those in Sombra who have gone fully demonic, turning to the dark before they end their own existence.

The horned skulls are all that remains of those who did. Over the centuries, Duke Haures has even sentenced those that betrayed him to the lost shadows. Some of these remains belong to the demons he executed. Others are demons who didn't just fade away, but sought out a quicker and more brutal end.

Sometimes, immortality isn't a promise. Forever can be a threat. Over my first millennium, I existed with the hope that I would someday find my one true mate. How long would I have simply endured for the idea of the female who might be mine? Ten centuries? Twenty? The doppelseers passed *thirty* before they claimed Tandy… would I have grown tired of the monotony and ended up just another skull on the edge of the ash fields?

I don't know. I can't say. But as I ignore the skulls, focusing instead on what Dagon has found, I realize it doesn't matter. Forever has become something that I will cling to with my claws.

But how can I when it seems that it's slipping through my fingers like ash? Some unknown male snuck into our *home*. He took our child. My mate's anguished cry broke my heart; her tears scald me more than the heated rain falling from the sky.

In all my years, I've only seen a true rain fall in Nuit three times: once when I was a young demon; two days ago when Alana cried; and now. Only this time, it isn't a fluke. What started as a drizzle—a human word I'm familiar with from my time on Earth—has become more insistent, closer to the threatening downpour from the other day. It hisses and spits and splashes as it finds a patch of lava beneath the ash. Minutes pass—

horrible, terrible minutes where my child is missing, and I'm helpless to do anything right now other than chase after her—and the rain doesn't stop.

Just like the prophecy foretold, the fires of Sombra are being dampened by the unusual water, the rain continuing to fall even as anger has seemingly dried my mate's eyes.

She is glaring at the print Dagon found in the muddy ash. Because of the drizzle, the ground has left evidence of the male who snuck out through the back of our house with our hopefully slumbering babe; though the rain tells us it was most likely otherwise. Dagon followed them here, to the edge of the shadows, and is quiet as he waits for her to come to the same conclusion that he already has about the owner of these footsteps.

A male. A *human* male.

This unknown human male is the only one who could have made these footprints. First of all, they are from shoes, something most Sombra demons don't bother with. Large, flat boots that dug deep into the dirt as though the male was heavy enough to sink into the ground. A Sombra demon would shift to their shadows if attempting to be stealthy; we wouldn't leave prints at all.

More than that, I can *smell* him.

The scent is distinctly human, and I agree that he must be a male. There's a darkness to his scent, though, and he stinks of despair and terror and, at the same time, *hope*.

What does that mean? I don't know, and neither does Dagon.

As for Shannon—

"You're sure?" my mate asks at last, her voice shaky, her emotions raw. She may have my essence, but her human nose is nowhere near as powerful as a Sombra demon's, so I'm not surprised she doubts Dagon. "A guy? A human guy? Not a woman?" She shudders out a breath. "It can't be a chick. What the hell am I saying? That Kennedy took Alana? Or Billie? No."

"I can promise you that it wasn't Sierra, either, as the red moon kept my mate and I too busy to even leave Glaine's home," Dagon confirms. "Sammael and his mate went to stay with the mage. Even if these prints didn't suggest a human male, all of the human females in Sombra are bonded. The red moon would've left them too distracted to do this."

Distracted…

"*Fuck* being distracted. I should've known." Shannon slaps her hand down on the wet ash angrily, spraying it over our feet. "My daughter was in danger. I should've *known*."

I wish I had. To protect Alana, to save Shannon from suffering, knowing that someone has stolen our spawn…

Dagon steps out of the way of her justified anger.

"If you had ever experienced mate sickness, you would know that sometimes the gods make these choices for us."

"Your gods, maybe," retorts Shannon. "Not mine. Not Mal's. The gods who are looking out for us would never want us to get laid so badly that they'd risk our baby." She rubs the wet ash on the shadow coverings I wove for her before rising up from her crouch. The way her ridge-free brow furrows… my strong mate has forced back the worst of her fear in favor of planning her next move. "This is the last print, right? And you found the first one outside the back of our house?"

That's what Dagon explained to us as he led Shannon and me to the outskirts of Nuit. Just in case, Apollyon and Glaine were going house to house, seeing if any other villagers could tell us where Alana was, while Loki and Sammael—the only two mages in our clan—were using their magic to attempt to locate our spawn.

As a hunter, Dagon used his skill to track the male responsible for taking Alana. I had hoped that, when he brought us to the edge of shadows, lined by the skulls… I had hoped that he left Nuit, heading for a neighboring village.

But as Shannon peers at the dark shadows with a clever eye, I suddenly understand that it won't be as easy as chasing after him before he can join another demon clan.

Whether or not Dagon's human mate is as crafty as mine, he doesn't understand the harm in telling Shannon, "Yes. And every indication is that he brought your spawn into the shadows with him."

Dagon's Sierra is with spawn now. If anyone ever threatened their child, the hunter would do whatever it took to get her back—just like I shall.

I am an artist, yes. But I've also learned from Nox, trained with some of the other hunters in Nuit, and am filled with Shannon's essence. That's why, when Dagon admits that the male brought Alana with him into the inky black shadows, I expect Shannon to march right toward them.

She does. Without the sneaks she instructed Loki to conjure for her, without any other covering than my shadows, my wee human mate is careful to avoid the skulls even as she heads for the wall of shadows at the end of Nuit.

My mate is connected to me, through our essence exchange, our bond, and the shadows I gave her so that she wasn't walking around the village square completely bare. Even then, she seems surprised when I dash in front of her, holding up my hands, blocking her from marching straight into the darkest shadows in our realm.

Shannon recovers quickly. Fisting her hands on her hips, she glares up at me. "Every minute we're dicking around out here is another minute some whack job has Alana. I can't let that happen, Mal. I'm going to get her. If you guys don't want to come, that's fine. I'll go by myself."

"You know I will follow you anywhere—"

"Then what are you waiting for? Chop chop. Let's fucking go."

I glance at Dagon.

He shakes his head, red eyes blazing back at me.

He doesn't think Shannon should go into the shadows. Of course not. When this is the place where Sombra demons come to die… it scares the essence out of me to think of my Shannon getting lost in the dark.

But we can't abandon Alana, either—

Taking my quiet as my agreement, she darts around me. My heart leaps as I close my arms around her. I'm in my solid form. I nearly swallow her whole in my embrace, but I can't just let her go. If I do, I'll never see her again.

I know it down to my bones. At the very least, we go together. But if we can go prepared… whoever stole our spawn won't stand a chance.

I want to explain that to my mate. However, before I can, she wiggles in my hold. "Mal. What are you… no. I have to get her!"

"We will," I promise.

"Then let me go. I told you. We're wasting time here!"

"Shannon," rumbles Dagon. "You cannot go on your own."

"You think I'm an idiot? I know that. And I'm not going on my own. I have Malphas. My very own goddamn shadow. He's coming with me. Right, Mal?" Turning in my hold, her eyes search my face, head tilted up so that she can meet mine even as the rain tracks down her cheeks. Rain… or are those more tears? "Babe? We're not going to just stand here and let him have her. Right?"

I look over Shannon's head, meeting Dagon's flat stare again.

He grits his teeth, upper fangs digging into his flesh. Like me, he shifted to his solid form when the sensation of the rain falling through our shadows became too much to bear. "You don't know what you're asking. I led a human female into the shadows once. We nearly didn't survive the journey."

Dagon is the new target of Shannon's pointed stare. "But did you die?" she demands.

His expression turns confused. "I am a Sombra demon. I am immortal. The shadows nearly ended me… but here I stand before you."

"Exactly! That's my point. You're not dead. You made it out."

"Well, yes—"

"What about the human?" Shannon interrupts. "She made it out, too. That's what you said. *We* nearly didn't survive. If she could do it, so can I."

Dagon's fierce red eyes shadow over. "Susanna is

the reason I survived. She saved my life in the shadows."

Shannon's vindication slams into me. "See? Wait — hang on. Susanna? Like, the duke's mate?"

"Yes."

"Then there you go. If she survived whatever is in there, why can't I? And if I can't? At least I died trying to get my baby back."

Every ounce of me… every ounce of who Malphas was, who he is, and who he's become since I took Shannon Crewes's essence and willingly gifted her mine… every last part of me wants to bellow at the idea that there could ever be another moment in time when I existed but Shannon didn't. A thousand years waiting for her was enough. I can't ever go back to that.

And yet… I suddenly understand that, if I stop her from going after the male who stole Alana… she might still exist, but she'll never be *my* Shannon again.

There is only one thing to do.

"You need coverings," I tell her. "More than my shadows since they might not hold inside of there. For your body. For your feet. And one of Loki's light spells to help guide our path. Once we have those—"

"You'll let me go after Alana?"

"No, my mate," I say before following with a vow with as much solemnity as I had the night I made my mate's promise to my Shannon: "I will go with you to find our daughter."

"We'll go together? Really?"

Her hope burns inside of me, even hotter than the rain scalding my back. And the idea that she might have doubted her mate…

I tuck my pointer finger under her chin, lifting her face again so she can see the promise in mine. "We will find her. We will bring her home again. I vow it."

And nothing will stop us.

CHAPTER 13
FARIPOZ

SHANNON

The shadows.

Why did it have to be in the shadows?

That's all Sombra is. Fire and magic and black shadows everywhere you look. The ash under our feet is a mix of black, white, red, and grey, while the lava pools add shades of orange to the color scheme. In other parts of the realm—the capital city, in particular—you can see different colors. Mavro is blue, for example, and full of flowers that would turn to ash in a village like ours.

I always knew that Nuit is one of the furthest villages on the outskirts of Sombra. We live here because it's been Mal's home for more than a thousand years. While some demons move from clan to clan—or even to other demon realms—my kindhearted, gentle demon artist had a loyalty to where he was born.

But the *edge* of Sombra's shadows…

Malphas wants to protect me. He always does, but I see it now. In obvious ways, like how he physically moves himself to keep me from running right into the shadows, but in more subtle actions, like the way he keeps nudging any of the demon skulls surrounding us deeper into the ash so that I don't see them.

As if I can *miss* them.

I know what this is. This deep, dark, impossibly black wall of shadows whose entire existence is a warning to the villagers that live within its reach. It's not just the beginning of the end of the world. It's a place where no sane demon can survive for long.

It's a place they go to *die*.

After hearing the stories from Kennedy about her time in there with a fully demonic Loki, I told myself that I'd never go inside of the shadows myself. There's no reason for me to. I'm not a hunter, and Mal's eyes have never gone white; a sure sign that a demon has lost all their control. Even hunters rarely go more than a few steps inside. The prey beasts that they capture for the village lurk on the edges on purpose, as though even they are trying to escape what's inside of the shadows.

But some unknown human dick kidnapped Alana. For whatever reasons he had—whoever the hell *he* is —he crept into our house through the back while Mal and me were indisposed, stole my daughter, and headed right toward the shadows. Dagon swears it. He points out all the boot prints he found that back up his theory, and by the time he's done, I realize I don't care. He says some guy brought Alana into the shadows with him. Fine. Then that's where I'm going.

I thought that Mal would be right beside me. He's my mate. Though, as a Sombra demon, he insists on serving as my shadow, when it comes to our relationship, we go together. After the misstep he made, hiding Duke Haures's visits—whether he had the best of intentions or not—I never thought he'd do something like this again.

But he did. He stopped me, and though I know I'll never turn on my one true love, at that moment, I swore I felt my heart crack.

Malphas is the only one I can truly trust. The only one who understands what I'm going through. Not just because he has my essence and I have his, either. But because this is his daughter who's been taken, too, and he wants her returned to us at desperately as I do.

I *know* that. To the marrow of my bones, I believe that… and that's why I nearly broke to think he would rather let someone run off with our child than face the shadows.

I was right. I never should've doubted my mate, even if the moment was a fleeting one. After all, Mal was right, too. I needed to be prepared. Shoes. I needed shoes. Real clothing. We don't know what kind of magic works in the thick, heavy shadows, but between Loki and Sammael, I have two mages in Nuit who might be able to help us.

So, against my better judgment, I hurry back to the house to get everything we might need. Malphas runs with me, and I can tell from the tightness of his muscles that he honestly expected me to ignore him and possibly sacrifice myself by facing the shadows on my own before we were ready.

I send pure love down our bond. Even if it's just the two of us against the rest of the world, if I know one thing, it's this: Mal will always, always do what he thinks is best for me. I'm his mate. Sometimes, I need to let him.

We go in through the back. Within minutes, I've pulled on a fresh change of clothes. I throw my hair up in a ponytail, then stab my feet into a pair of sneakers. Mal tugs on a pair of actual tanned leathers—and if I wasn't in the middle of a nervous fucking breakdown, I might muse on what kind of shadow animal the tanners must have used to create pants like that—before keeping the rest of him bare.

Together, we make the mistake of heading out through the front. And maybe it's not a mistake—maybe, like everyone else that happens in the shadows, it was *meant* to be—because, waiting for us outside of our home, is about half of the village.

It's still raining. Enough of it falls that, no matter how hot Sombra is, they're… if not wet, at least damp. Malphas told me that the rain stings against a demon's skin. It's not all that pleasant for a human, either.

And, yet, here they all are. A lump lodges in my throat. I swallow it roughly.

Because, nearest to the porch, I see my friends and their mates. Kennedy and Billie, Sierra and Hope, even Tandy… they're all here, offering their support while also waiting for me to tell them what the hell has been going on since my scream broke the quiet earlier.

I firm my jaw. Raising my voice, I say, "Dagon followed tracks into the shadows at the end of Nuit. Of Sombra. I don't know who did it, but some guy… a *human* guy… took Alana. He took my *baby*. I'm going in there and I'm getting her back."

I don't have time for questions. I've given an update, and every moment I'm in Nuit, that's a moment that I don't have Alana back in my arms.

Grasping for Malphas's hand, craving that connection, *needing* it, I'm ready to start dashing back to the edge of the shadows when someone calls out to me.

"I'm coming with you."

I would know that voice anywhere. From the friendly greetings when I'd stop in at Turn the Page after my trip to The Beanery, to all the days we sat talking in the EL, watching over Alana, marveling over our lives and our mates… I know that voice.

And I know exactly why she makes that offer: because she loves my daughter as her own, just as she loves me as her friend. Of course Kennedy would offer.

I have to refuse. I *have* to.

"What? No. Ken, no. It won't be safe."

"I know. Believe me, I know. But you've never been in there before. I have."

"Yeah, but—"

"No buts. Loki will come with us. He spent over a hundred *years* in those terrible shadows. He'll help, too. Won't you?"

She turns to her mate, looking up at him through the fringe of her lashes. With her soft honey-blonde hair and heart-shaped face, I can't imagine anyone telling her no. Especially not her mate… but he has to. She's super pregnant. He can't risk her—

"Of course, I will, my heart," grates Loki. "I have magic now, and the experience of spending long years in the dark. If you want to join the hunt, I will join it alongside you."

"Hang on. Hunt?" I echo. "I'm not hunting—"

"But we are," murmurs Mal, squeezing my fingers. "We are hunting the ruthless human who might hurt our innocent spawn. Hunting him is exactly what we must do."

He's right. Obviously, he's right.

And though Loki is a born mage, with the tell-tale purple eyes, a hundred years as a lost demon has turned him into an even more ruthless hunter. That can help us. So can his magic. I'd let Loki join us in a heartbeat, but Kennedy… I can't. She's so close to having her own child—

As though she knows exactly what I'm thinking, she says, "You would do it for me. If it were my baby… I know you would, Shannon."

She's right, too.

"Okay." I give in if only because I know, no matter what, Loki will put Kennedy's safety before anything else. So long as he's with her, she's untouchable. I one hundred percent believe that. "But only if you're ready. I'm leaving now."

"We're coming with you, too," adds Billie, gesturing at her chest, then at Glaine's. "We've survived the shadows before. And, don't forget, Glaine has his sword."

"I also have Duke Haures's orders to see that the spawn is unharmed while I am in Nuit," Glaine says, shocking the shit out of me.

Then again, maybe that revelation shouldn't be so surprising. After all, Alana is supposedly the child of a prophecy that might lead to the end of this world as we know it. Who knows what would happen if she was harmed or… or *worse*… before the prophecy came to pass?

No. *No.* Nothing will happen to her because, instead of waiting for someone else to offer to come with us, I start tugging Mal away from the house. If they want to come, come. Whatever. The more the freaking merrier at this point, so long as they're willing to help me get my daughter back.

I get two steps before I discover that Glaine's pronouncement isn't the biggest shock I've gotten in the last couple of seconds—or that I need to be careful what I wish for.

Otherwise, I just might get it.

The more the merrier…

"The human women must all accompany the first," intones Lucian, his voice deep and his words clear.

The first? Does he mean Alana or me? Because I'm not the first. That's Susanna… unless it's something else he's referring to. Like, oh, being the first human woman to procreate with a Sombra demon?

Tandy lays her arm on the crook of Lucian's elbow. "Even me?"

His tone turns regretful as he says, "Yes. Even you, dear one. Your mates are, of course, welcome to join you. Damien and I will be there to keep Tandy safe from that which might hunt us in return."

Hope looks up at Sammael. "I've been in there before. It was terrifying, but I was alone."

"And I was in chains, doing everything I could to get back to you. Now you'll never be alone, Hope. We cannot defy the doppelseers. You'll go, and I'll go with you."

Sierra shrugs. "Well, count me in. You, too?"

Dagon tucks his mate against his side, red eyes blazing out of his solid face. A hint of water dots his ridged brow. His long hair is shoved behind him as he nods. "I know what the boot prints belonging to the human look like. I don't like the idea of you going in there with our spawn, but I would've offered my help in tracking either way. Now I can keep you safe and out of this blasted rain at the same time."

There's that lump in my throat again. Shit. I'm getting even more emotional, and for a totally different reason this time. I… I don't know what to say. Sure, Lucian made it clear that we have to go—and I can only imagine what it is he has seen that has him sure he has to risk the mate he and his mate waited *three* thousand years for but even if he hadn't… they would've come. I know it.

We're our own clan within a clan. Alana being born without shadows of her own doesn't mean a damn thing to them. Neither does her being the child of the prophecy… they want to help her because she's an innocent child, and because she's mine and Mal's.

And I will never, ever forget it.

As a group, Dagon takes us back the way we came. I have to restrain myself, resisting the urge to take off so that I can feel like I'm doing *something*. It's only as we've returned to the bleached skulls and the damp ash that I realize that running into the shadow is about as far as my plan goes.

I'm okay with it, but I have twelve other people—

humans and demons—that I feel responsible for. We need a plan.

And, as strange as it seems, we get one from the usually quiet, always prophetic second doppelseer.

Speaking for the first time all day that I've heard, Damien suddenly intones softly, "Float on the air, lead the way."

Huh?

Obviously, his twin has some idea of what Damien means. While I'm confused as hell, Lucian sucks in a breath as he follows his brother's gaze somewhere behind the rest of us. "Faripoz."

I turn, doing a double-take when I notice the glowing white… shit. I don't know what it is. It looks like the outline of a winged *thing*, the striking glow surrounding it the only way to tell its shadows apart from the impenetrable black shadows at the end of Sombra.

It flutters, the wings moving so quickly it's hard to make out its shape, but as the word 'flutter' pops into my worried brain, I do recognize what I'm looking at.

It's a butterfly.

I blink.

Sombra has butterflies?

Now, I haven't lived in Sombra long. Only a couple of months since I gave birth, though I've had to make pretty frequent trips so that Azazel could check me out during the pregnancy. I've never once seen a butterfly. To be fair, the only animal I've seen is

Kennedy's pet squirrel-cat-looking shadow animal, Freya, and if I wasn't shitting bricks over my missing baby, I'd marvel over witnessing Sombra's version of a butterfly.

But then, over the roar of panic inside my ears, it hits me what Damien said. Something about *lead the way…*

I clutch Mal's arm. "Do we follow the butterfly?" Hope swells inside my chest. This… this might work. Lucian saw it, right? So did Damien… this *has* to work. "Will it lead us to Alana?"

The ridges over his brow scrunch together, water dripping slowly down his solid skin, beads of moisture welling in the smile creases above his upper lip. He's not smiling now, though; concerned and confused, he narrows his golden eyes on the butterfly. "What is this creature?"

"One of the faripoz," repeats Lucian. "And a sure sign that the spawn is in control of her own fate."

SHANNON

I don't know what the hell that's supposed to mean. Honestly? It doesn't matter. All it takes is one of the creepy psychic twins confirming that we're supposed to follow the butterfly into the shadows before I'm dipping into the darkness.

Join me if you want. Lucian says we're all supposed to go together? Sure. Let's go.

Just like I figured, Mal is right behind me, hovering near me, though he's instinctively shifted to his shadow form again to match my step without accidentally bumping into me or knocking me over. Sometimes I forget that my mate is more than seven feet tall, with the muscular bulk to match such a build. He's always so careful with me, but the way we're running blindly into the pitch-black shadows, if I fall under his foot, he could really hurt me.

It wouldn't be on purpose. Mal loses his ever-loving mind if I so much as stub my toe in his presence. All the more reason for him to fade to his transparent shadow form so that he can keep up with my pace without the threat of his big body knocking into me.

I can't tell if it's easier for him to navigate just how fucking dark it is in here. It's cooler, too, which is saying something when we live in a demon realm made of fire, lava, and ash. Cooler means it's a balmy seventy instead of a dry ninety-five degrees Fahrenheit, but after getting used to the heat of Nuit, I shiver as the shadows envelop me.

There are bones beneath the ash under my feet. It's dark, but I can kinda see where I'm going, and the bleached white femurs and who-knows-what-else poking through are definitely hard to miss. I mean, I thought the horned skulls were bad. Crunching on something I can't exactly see… nope. This is worse. So much worse.

Only one moon rises high in the black sky, providing some light. Normally, I'd say that the reddish, shadow-filled world turns their main moon the same color. Now that I've seen what a blood-red moon looks like? It's more a pale orange than anything our first few steps before it takes on the shadows. It's still bright, still giving us enough light that I'm not completely blind, but the moon's a fore-boding dark color that's outlined against the sky the same way those butterflies gleam against the shadows.

Mal's shadowy hand ghosts over my arm, brushing against my sunflower tattoo. I jolt, his emotions—fear and worry and a determination to get our baby back—echoing mine as we touch. Our bond sings out as I assure Mal that I'm here, that we're in this together, even with our friends joining in on the chase.

We left the drizzle outside of the shadows. That's the one good thing about willingly entering the dark. As though the shadows themselves are a living, breathing thing, we're consumed by them. A sliver of moonlight high over our heads is the only illumination we have. It's enough to make out vague shapes; other-wise, all I can see are the glowing eyes that belong to the other Sombra demons.

Gold. Red. Purple. Green.

One of the purple-eyed demons does something. He shifts his body, and when he's done, an orb about the size of a baseball is hovering over one of his palms. A faint white light emanates from the orb, providing enough of a glow that I recognize its holder as Loki.

Kennedy is holding tightly to his bicep. I'm sure he conjured the light so that his heavily freaking preg-nant mate can see where she's going, but I don't give a shit. It helps the rest of us, too, and since we're a (hopefully) lucky thirteen, I'll take it.

The last thing I want is for one of my friends and their demon mates to find trouble in the shadows while helping me search for my daughter. Well, no… the last thing I want is to get lost in the dark and never see Alana again, but I'll feel guilty as hell if anyone else gets hurt.

Loki is at home in the shadows; after all, he spent a hundred years inside of them as a demonic beast. Even Kennedy spent her first few months in Sombra in here because this where Loki first brought her after he stole her away to the demon world with him. Of course, Kennedy's also told me about the giant black shadow bear that nearly ate her so… I'd like to avoid one of those if we can.

And then there's Billie. Before she arrived in Nuit with Glaine, the two of them journeyed from the capital in Mavro, halfway across Sombra, until the creepy, psychic twins picked them up and basically gave them a ride closer to our village. Part of their trip took them into the shadows along the edge of Sombra, where a different, fully demonic Sombran decided he was going to take Billie away from her grumpy soldier mate.

Glaine wasn't a big fan of the idea. That's how I found out the guard I've loathed ever since he threatened Mal outside of Turn the Page carries an enchanted sword that can kill immortal demons.

Luckily for us, he's on our side. If anything in these shadows targets Billie, they'll be dead before we know it. Glaine already has his sword pulled out of the shadow pocket where he usually keeps it stored. I catch glimmers of it out of the corner of my eye whenever Loki's orb glances off of it.

Another plus? The light does a good job of warning some of the white-eyed shadow critters back. Dagon assures us that all of the white pinpricks peering out at us from the pitch-black darkness are prey beasts. The kind of slow, skittish shadow animals that make up all of the questionable meat that we eat in Sombra. I like to think they're, like, shadow chicken and shadow beef, but considering one of the delicacies is ungez like Kennedy's pet, Freya… I'd rather not see what I'm chowing down on as the 'before'.

I already refuse to eat ungez out of solidarity with the adorable squirrel-cat. If I discover that bronwyll is a cute raccoon-beaver or something, I might go veggie after all…

The predators claim the territory deeper into the shadows. If the butterfly leads us that far, that's something else to worry about. Part of me hopes that one of those arkoda-bear things finds that prick who thought he could take Alana. But when I realize that means my baby would be at the mercy of a mindless shadow beast, I don't know what's worse: being in the clutches of her abductor or a wild animal.

Either way, my sweet, innocent baby would be stuck with a monster.

She's in here. Dagon followed the human male's tracks into the shadows. Even Lucian and Damien are convinced we have to go this way to find her. We just have to follow the butterfly—which would've been so much fucking easier if the butterfly leading the way didn't suddenly *disappear* on us.

Even worse, I may be shit when it comes to directions, but I know I saw half of a thigh bone sticking out of the ash, perched against one of the burnt trees that hide in the shadows. When I see it again about ten minutes later, the same angle, the same divots dug out of the bone as though a pair of violent claws went at it, I kick it.

Losing the butterfly was bad enough. It winked out right before I noticed the bone. That's probably why I was so pissed that I kicked it in the first place, but *fuck* it felt good to get out some of my aggression.

It's only mildly better than dealing with the shame that I allowed my baby to be taken.

So the red moon basically roofied us. So Nuit was supposed to be safe, just like there shouldn't have been any human guys in here. As far as I can tell, there's only been one: Connor, Amy's abusive douchebag of an ex. And since Amy confided in me that Nox brought Connor to the shadows to keep him away from his mate and, you know, *kill* him, I highly doubt he was around to nab my baby.

Besides, Connor's abandonment in Sombra was almost twenty years ago. I've been in the shadows for a half an hour, tops, and I feel like I'm losing my mind. Connor couldn't survive, right?

Does it matter?

When Alana needs me… needs Mal… does it matter who fucking took her?

I want my baby back!

I thrust my fingers through my hair, shoving it out of my face as the thigh bone soars into the dark reaches of the shadows, landing with a muffled thump against the dry ash. "We followed the stupid butterfly. We've gone in fucking circles. What are we supposed to do now?"

Dagon crouches down to the ash in front of him.

Sierra scoots closer to him, her calf bumping his knee. "What are you looking for?"

"Tracks," he says, answering his mate. "I've been using Loki's spell to search for the same boot print. The human male came this way, but I don't see any more prints."

"Where was the last one you saw?" That's Glaine. The soldier twists his wrist, keeping himself—and his sword—ready. "If the faripoz has left us, we might have to backtrack and find the way the human has gone with the spawn."

"The faripoz has done its purpose," confirms Lucian.

"For now," adds Damien. "Until the wicked wind

whips it along a different path, the innocent calling out for its familiar."

What?

Another prophecy? Or some more gibberish that makes sense to him and no one else?

I bite down, trying not to lose my ever-loving shit. Taking out my frustrations on the riddle-speaking doppelseer next would be a bad idea, I know that, but when he says shit like that… when he's not helpful at all… it's not that easy.

Good thing I have my mate. Mal brushes up against me, his touch tethering me. He's so sure that I can do this. That I, too, can do *anything.* That together we can find Alana… and no way in hell am I going to disappoint him.

Through my gritted teeth, I say, "Please, Dagon. Do you remember?"

He nods. "This way."

Loki makes sure that Kennedy is tucked next to Sammael and Hope before he surges forward, lending more light to the hunter.

We just have to retrace our footsteps and figure out where we lost the kidnapper's print. He can't just disappear, right? Humans don't fly. Portals don't work in the restless dark that marks the edge of this demon world. Sammael proved that when he tried to move further ahead, hoping to catch the unknown human guy before he got too far. He couldn't even summon one. It's up to us to track him—

—but it's im-fucking-*possible*.

He shouldn't have been able to disappear. He *shouldn't*. But when Dagon goes back and finds the last boot print he saw, he wasn't wrong. It's the *last* boot print, angled away from the path. In between one step and the next, the guy who made them has seemed to vanish.

Worse, there's a… a *wall* there. Loki's light shows a patch of black that is so impossibly dark, it's not a shadow. You can't see through it. If there's something on the other side, I can't tell. Wherever the kidnapper's taken her, I can't follow him. I try. I run to the ends of it, as far as where Loki's light illuminates the ash and the burnt trees. I see more of the same behind the wall, but I know… I just *know*… that I would be wasting my time going around it.

I have to go *through* it—and I can't.

And that means I can't go after Alana.

CHAPTER 15
FREYA SAVES THE DAY

SHANNON

"**N**o." It's a whisper first before the next one rises in pitch again and again until I'm shouting as I run back to where everyone is still standing there, unsure what to do while my world falls apart *again*. "No, no, no, no, *no*!"

I throw a punch at the wall. Proving my point, I hit it, but as though it's made of rubber, my hand comes flying back at me.

It's no shadow. It's a goddamn sideways trampoline!

"What the hell do we do now?" I don't expect anyone to have the answer. Malphas is already moving in, ready to embrace me so that, when I shatter once more, I don't end up among the bones in the ash. I need him, but I need someone to know what to do.

Because giving up? That isn't an option.

"We go forward. This is the way."

Doesn't Lucian think that I would if I could? "How? Look!" I hit it again, my fist bouncing off once more. "It's a wall."

"It's a block."

I don't have time for semantics. "There has to be a way—"

He has to know. He has to have seen something else. I heard Tandy ask during one of the tense lulls when I thought I lost the butterfly earlier, and all he murmured to his mate was that our clan will see the prophecy through to the end… whatever *that* means.

But how? How can we do that if something is stopping us? And why, as I fist my hands, searching for something, *anything*, to give me an idea to move forward, do I get the feeling that it's not just the shadows fucking with us?

That someone is helping the human steal Alana— or that the human is stealing her for someone else?

I don't know, but suddenly my words cut short as I notice something that no one else does.

Moments ago, I had turned from the wall… block… *thing*. In my panic, I'm looking at everyone gathered, hoping that someone will have a better idea than Lucian. There are plenty of us—because Lucian said we all had to come as if *that*'s helped at all—but the women give me apologetic looks. The demons all seem to think that Malphas should be doing something to calm me down.

How can he when, through our bond, I can tell he's as close to freaking out as I am?

They don't understand. We're her parents, so of course this is affecting us. I have no illusions. Kennedy is here for me. Maybe even Billie, since she swore she would never go back into the shadows again after that feral demon attacked her and Glaine, but she's here. Sierra would've probably come because I needed Dagon, but everyone else? If Lucian hadn't used his position as the doppelseer to have all of the human-demon-mated pairs join us, there wouldn't have been a reason for them to come.

Or is there?

I don't know, but frustrated that our journey is already stalled, I'm staring at them all when I notice that one of the shadow creatures has grown bold enough to approach our group.

No, not just approach.

One of the creatures is running right toward two of us.

I see its eyes. Glowing white and barely a foot off of the ash, they move like a pair of headlights on a child's toy car. For a moment, I'm distracted as I watch it, expecting it to veer off. When it doesn't... when it becomes clear it's actually targeting *one* of us, I call out her name.

"Kennedy! Watch out!"

The creature leaps. Flying higher than I ever would've expected it to be able to, it launches itself at Kennedy before landing perfectly on her shoulder.

Perfectly, like it's made the same move a hundred times.

Perfectly, like she knows her mistress.

"Freya!" Kennedy nuzzles the ungez's shadowy fur as the squirrel-cat chirps up at her. "You naughty girl… what are you doing? You know better than to follow us into the shadows. You could've been gobbled up!"

She's not wrong. In Sombra, ungez are the most common prey animals. In fact, Kennedy told me that she kept Freya as a pet after Loki hunted the ungez, hoping to feed her to Kennedy. It's way too dangerous for her to be in here.

So why is she?

I mean, I probably should've known. When neither Loki nor Kennedy reacted until I shouted, I should've known it wasn't just any white-eyed shadow creature tracking them.

But that doesn't explain what Freya is doing here.

One more nuzzle and, suddenly, she's leaping back to the ash. Her tail whips wildly. Her pointed nose sniffs. A moment later, she moves directly in front of the wall of impenetrable shadow.

She chitters, then waits.

What is she—

She squeaks, more insistent this time, then waits again.

I can't believe this—

She rears back on her hind legs as another pair of glowing white eyes peek out at her from beneath the wall.

From *beneath* the wall.

No. It couldn't be that easy, could it?

Freya touches noses with the other ungez. Because that's what it is. As it shimmies its way out, it's clear that I'm looking at Freya's twin.

She looks back at Kennedy, preening a little.

"What a good girl," she breathes out.

The other ungez squeaks, then turns and burrows its way back under the wall. Freya scampers over to Kennedy, rubbing her ankle before strolling over to the spot where her friend disappeared.

Then, a heartbeat later, Freya is also gone.

I don't know how much room is down there, but there must be enough for her to turn around, sticking her face out from inside the gap. She chitters once more, eyes flashing. I get the vibe she's telling us *silly humans* in ungez, that we're taking too long, because she snaps her dainty fangs, turns around again, and vanishes.

"Freya!" calls Kennedy.

A faint squeak from a little further in the distance tells us that, wherever the ungez went, she's done it. She's found a way around the block.

Hope… the emotion, not the person… it's a delicate, fragile thing. Part of me doesn't want to believe that Kennedy's pet followed us all the way through the shadows to help. It's so damn fantastical… but I mated a monster. Before Sammael returned to his demon form, Hope was fated to a phantom. Billie was grabbed by a guard.

And Kennedy bonded to a beast in these same shadows that Freya once called home.

This is real life. Even when I look around, see the demons, and admit that I've stumbled into a fantasy romance with a kind, sexy demon lead, it's *real*… but in my new, real life, why can't a tiny black squirrel-cat with glowing white eyes save the day like Sombra's version of freaking *Lassie*?

"I'm going," I announce to the stunned group. Freya is small, but the ash moves. It's not packed together like dirt. If I dig a little and wiggle, I can follow her.

This is the way… that's what Lucian said.

I look at the stone-faced seer, arching an eyebrow.

He nods.

Yes!

"We will all go," he says. "One at a time. And if we are warded away again, now we will know how to get past it."

"Because of Freya," Kennedy beams.

"We will all go." That's my mate agreeing with Lucian. "And I will go first."

What? No. I was going to go first.

My head swivels, searching for my mate's golden eyes. "Mal—"

Right there, he lays his hands on my shoulders. "I will always follow you, my flower. But, this once, I need you to be the one who comes second."

When it came to me throwing myself to the ash, I didn't care. But now that Mal wants to go…

"I don't know. What if there's some kind of monster waiting for us on the other side?"

His demon eyes gleam. "There was a time you thought *I* was a monster."

True. I mean, in my defense, anyone would think the same when a seven-foot-tall shadow demon with glowing eyes, pointed ears, horns, and a freaking base-ball club between their thighs popped out of an inter-dimensional portal into their apartment.

But my demon mate is so much more than that. He's kindhearted. Devoted. Loyal. The best lover I've ever had, the sweetest companion, and Alana's father.

How can I stop him from going after our daughter and protecting his mate?

I don't argue with him. And maybe everyone else expects me to, but there's no time for that.

Squeezing his side, I send a pulse of pure love down our bond. "Be careful, okay? And I'll be right behind you."

"I'll shout when it's clear," he promises.

He holds true to his word. After what feels like the

longest three minutes of my life, eventually I hear Mal calling my name. Assuming that means it's safe for me to follow him, I do.

I understand immediately what took so long. Malphas had to dig furrows into the ash to fit his body; shadow form or not. As big, tall, and bulky as he is, he's left a path that's tight yet easy enough for me to take. In less than two, he's taking my ash-covered hand in his, tugging me out of the hole and pulling me to my feet so that he can embrace me.

One by one, the rest of our group crawls on their bellies in the ash. Loki brings up the rear while Kennedy nibbles nervously on her dirty thumb. Her pregnant belly gave her a little bit of trouble, and only having her mate behind her, talking her through it, led to her finishing the crawl.

Freya waits for Loki to check over his mate before she joins her human.

Rearing back on her hind legs, she chatters up at Kennedy.

She exhales. "Okay. Fine. You can stay. But if you see any threats, I want you to run back home. I know you can do it. You've already done enough."

Freya chitters, eyes flashing brighter than the orb that Loki conjured again, showing off that this side of the shadow block is exactly the damn same as the other.

Kennedy crouches down, meeting the ungez so

that she can ruffle her shadows. "I'll be alright. I have Loki."

Freya makes what I can only describe as a disbelieving scoff.

Seriously.

Kennedy laughs softly. "Behave, Freya. You're really being a naughty girl now that you helped."

"Okay. If no one else is going to say anything about this, I am. Kennedy, what the hell? You speak shadow rat?" Tandy asks, barely bothering to hide her amused yet incredulous tone.

"I've been trying to tell you guys all along," Kennedy says, pausing so that Freya can scamper up her body and settle around her neck like a shawl. "Ungez are really, really smart. And she's not a shadow rat, okay? She's more like a mix of a cat and a squirrel, thank you very much." Excitement suddenly creeps into her voice. "A squirrel-cat that just got us closer to finding Alana!" She points. "Look!"

A butterfly.

It's another butterfly.

Is it the same? No clue, but if we're supposed to follow the damn thing, it's such a relief to see it flapping away on the other side of the tight channel we just wormed our way through.

I laugh. Part relief, part that stubborn hope I'm allowing myself to cling to... I laugh, and I'm just glad the unfamiliar sound doesn't frighten the glowing butterfly away.

And then, after giving Freya a pat of gratitude of my own, I say, "Someone's gotta tell Apollyon that we're taking ungez off the menu. And Mal, baby? When we get Alana back, we're getting her a Freya of her own."

Because it's not an *if*.

It's a *when*.

CHAPTER 16

THR33PEAT REUNION

SHANNON

I had hoped that whatever was trying to keep us from following after Alana... the human guy... the Sombran gods... Fate... *whatever*... had given up once Freya taught us how to find ways around the blocks they're throwing up.

Sometimes we have to go under. Once, we had to shimmy through a 'crack' between two walls that nearly had Kennedy and Loki turning back until she figured out how to fit her belly through. It irked the hell out of me that the big demons could fit, though they had the added bonus of being able to turn to shadow and make themselves a little bit smaller. Meanwhile, all of us women are of different heights, different builds, different sizes, but it's her poor bump that keeps giving her trouble.

I'll give Kennedy credit. She's determined as hell. She refuses to admit if she's tired, and she won't slow us down. If she starts to drag, she allows Loki to carry her before insisting he let her down again so she can leave him free to use his orb to help guide the way.

I asked her why after she struggled with the upright 'crack'. Her answer didn't surprise me. Though her child will be the *second* halfling born in this age, she doesn't know what to expect from them. She's helping me because we're basically family now, and if the time comes that she needs the favor returned, she wants to make sure me and Mal will be there.

Of course we will, but those pregnancy hormones are no joke. If this is something Kennedy has to do, I'm not about to tell her no. Instead, I bite my tongue when she takes a little longer to maneuver her way around the blocks, all while reminding myself that we're going as fast as we can—and, if it wasn't for Kennedy's bond with Freya in the first place, I'd still be beating the crap out of the bouncy wall that blocked us about two hours ago.

There haven't been any obstructions for the last twenty minutes or so. Those are rough guesstimates since time doesn't quite exist in Sombra—especially in the dark shadows—but it seems long enough that I start hoping that we're getting closer. That they— whoever *they* are—have decided we're worthy, and we can catch up to Alana and her kidnapper before something else catches up to them *first*—

Suddenly a thunderous roar splits the darkness. It's so loud, I whimper, someone else gasps, and one of the other women shrieks in fright. The ground shakes. The air rattles. Smaller squawks and spooked chattering erupts in the echoes of the roar. The prey beasts leave rustling sounds in their wake as they try to run from whatever the hell made that noise.

—like, oh, *that*.

Shit, shit, shit, shit, shit!

My hands grab fearfully for my mate. His arm, his side, his shoulder… whatever part of him I can find beneath his shadows, I dig my fingers in and hold on tight.

Malphas wraps his arms around me, murmuring reassurances that I can't hear over my thudding heart.

"What the fuck was that?" I blurt out.

"Oh, no," moans Kennedy. Freya's wrapped around her mistress so tightly, the shadowy squirrel-cat has basically made herself into a scarf.

She didn't run, though, so good on her for that. If my legs weren't paralyzed by that roar, I might've.

"That wasn't an arkoda." It's Loki that answers, and after his experience living in these shadows, I believe him. I'm grateful, too. Arkodas are like the Sombra version of rabid grizzlies. No way we could get past one of them, and maybe I'm crazy for thinking of a search and rescue mission as, like, a quest to retrieve my daughter, but something tells me that we *have* to. "It's a huigitz."

Kennedy's forehead scrunches. She must be digging into Loki's essence to get a human reference for the shadow predator because, after a moment, she pales. "Ah, crap."

I don't like the sound of that. "Tell me, Ken. How bad is it?"

"Bad," is her breathless response. "Think 'moose meets lion', bad. It's gotta be eight feet high, at least, with antlers and a fuzzy mane. And teeth." She shudders, stroking Freya's shadowy fur. "So many teeth."

Wonderful.

"Fear not, Shannon." Lucian slips away from his twin and his mate, gliding over toward me and Mal before turning to address us all. "I have seen this."

"Great," snaps Billie. She started getting anxious after one of the last blocks, almost as though it finally hit her how far her and Glaine had traveled into the shadows. He's still holding his sword, while she's been clutching his arm as though she likes to walk connected to him, no gold chains required. "The doppelseer has watched all of us get gobbled up by a shadow monster."

"Not quite, Tandy's kin. Before we found our mate, the gods hid her from us. All we saw was red. But since she's accepted us both into her heart, her bedding, and her cunt—"

Tandy snorts, not an ounce of shame that her

psychic mate is sharing her business like that. "You flatterer, you."

His lips twitch just enough to break his serious expression for a heartbeat. He recovers quickly, though, before continuing where she interrupted him, "—we see more that involves our dear mate. And this… we have seen this."

One at a time, Lucian gestures at Tandy, then Billie, then Sierra.

Damien steps forward. Then, in that creepy voice he gets when he's reciting a prophecy, he says, *"Diamonds in my laugh, I shine too bright… make your pulse race under the neon lights… you talk big, I guess we'll see…"*

Kennedy gasps. Even as he stops, she hurriedly adds another line: "Can you keep up with a girl like me?"

What the—

"Kennedy? You've turned psychic on me now, too?"

"No! It's just… I recognized it. Those are lyrics to one of my favorite songs!"

Huh? "What are you talking about?"

"It's 'Ooh-Bop-Bop'," Sierra mumbles. "Thr33-peat's break-out hit single."

Oh. Well, that would explain it. I was never a fan of Thr33peat—though I adore the three individual members on their own just as they are without stanning them the way that Kennedy does, or how Hope is a huge follower of Whiskey Rose's career—and it's probably been a decade since I heard the bubblegum pop hit of my high school years.

Tandy slides her gaze over to Sierra. "You remember?"

Sierra pauses, then nods. "Yeah, I remember. I remember a lot from those days."

Tandy flinches.

Billie releases Glaine. "Oh, for fuck's sake. I've waited months for the two of you to finally grow a pair and hash this out."

"Bee, I don't think this is the time—"

She points at Sierra. "We're immortal, Sierra. We have nothing but time. And if your mates have seen something to do with us, with 'Ooh-Bop-Bop'? Then we can find the time." She jerks her thumb at Damien. "Listen. This one? He likes to speak in riddles, but sometimes he uses song lyrics in his prophecies. He did it for me with 'Heart Barely Used'. That's your song. 'Ooh-Bop-Bop' was ours. When we were a group."

"When we were friends," Tandy says softly before raising her voice. "Before I fucked up and betrayed you."

Sierra bites the corner of her mouth. "That's ancient history, Tan. We don't have to bring that up now. Not when Shannon and Malphas's baby needs us."

Tandy glances at Lucian. He nods at her, and I

know that whatever he's seen, this is *exactly* the time they need to hash this out.

"Listen. I've told you how it happened. How Jared lied to both of us… I thought that justified my behavior. It didn't, Sierra. It never did. I should've known better than to turn to him when *you* were the one I cared about. He was just a dick. You… you and Billie were my best friends."

"I told you I forgave you—"

Billie nudges Sierra.

Sierra glares at her, though she does amend it to: "I told you I would try. And I am. Jared… what the fuck do I care about Jared Turner when I have Dagon? My mate loves me. He'll never stray. I can trust him."

"You can trust me, too. Remember what Billie said. We've got nothing but time… and, if you're willing to give our friendship another try, I'd love to be Auntie Tandy to that baby you've got cooking."

Sierra's hand settles on her bump. For a moment, I think she's just going to blow off Tandy again—and I might throttle her if she does—but, instead, she gives her old friend the same smile that's graced the covers of nearly every single freaking magazine on Earth.

"Yeah," she says. "Yeah. Auntie Tandy… I'd like that."

Billie's poke becomes a proud pat on Sierra's arm. "So long as you remember that I get to be her godmother. And, yeah, maybe that means I'll have to be a *gods*mother in Sombra, but you know what I mean."

Sierra chuckles. "Yeah, Bee. I know."

Aw. I'd be lying if I said this scene wasn't super freaking heartwarming, but I'm impatient and worried and still need to get my daughter back so…

"What exactly did you see, Lucian?"

"The huigitz is a ferocious beast with only one weakness. Music. A three-part harmony expertly sung will serve as a lullaby, enabling us to get one step closer to retrieving Alana."

Retrieving Alana… here's hoping that he saw *that*, too.

Still, you have got to be shitting me. "Are you saying that the only way to get around it is if Sierra, Billie, and Tandy sing a song and put it to sleep?"

He nods. "We cannot risk getting too close to it. They can project their voices, and with their combined harmony, the huigitz will no longer be a threat."

Great. I'm going with it. At this point, I'll go with anything.

As long as it gets me my baby back.

I turn to the members of Thr33peat—and that's when I notice that the three of them are facing off, looking like a Thr33peat reunion in the middle of Sombra's shadows is the last thing any of them want.

Oh, come *on*.

"It's just one song. I'd do it, but Lucian said three-part harmony, and I can't hold a key in a freaking bucket. Please. For Alana."

Sierra steps forward. "You're right. It's just one song." She cracks her neck, rolling her head a few times before nodding. Then, to my amazement, she couches down a little, bending her knees and planting her palms on top of them.

Billie rolls her eyes, then moves to stand next to Sierra. Crossing her arms over her chest, she cocks a hip against Sierra's shoulder.

With a blinding grin, Tandy bounds over to them. Her arms get folded behind her head, a pout on her lips.

Kennedy starts flapping her hands in excitement. "Oh my god, oh my *god*. A Thr33peat reunion!"

Hope surges forward, standing next to her so the two have a front-row seat to what's about to happen. And I know that's exactly what they're thinking because Hope squeals. "I can't believe we're getting a private Whiskey Rose concert."

"It's better because it's *Thr33peat*!"

Hope doesn't argue. I guess she's just excited to see Sierra sing. Me? I'm just kinda hoping they can get on with it. Last thing I need right now is their squeals drawing this huigitz thing closer to us before they even get the chance to put it to sleep.

And that's when Tandy switches her pose, moving her hands from her head to her hips. "One."

Billie cocks her hip in the other direction, throwing one arm up in the air. "Two."

Sierra pops up, landing in a wide-legged stance. "Three."

There's no music. Honestly, there doesn't need to be. And as though a good twelve years haven't passed since they last performed this song together, Thr33-peat begin to sing—and, okay, they sound awesome a capella.

Hope and Kennedy cling to each other, dancing in place as they start the song.

When it's Tandy's turn to belt out the chorus, I actually find myself singing along a little under my breath, remembering more of the hit than I thought I did: "...one look, one shot, can't get enough... ooh-bop-bop, this is how we love..."

Kennedy gives me a warning look. Oh, right. Three-part harmony and Shannon sounds like a dying cat. Got it.

Halfway through the song, Loki and Dagon separate from the group. Within seconds, they're back, and the look of relief on their faces tells me that, holy shit, this actually worked!

Still, we wait until they finish their song, Kennedy finally losing the battle with herself as she sings out the last line with them. For a heartbeat, I worry that that might've been enough to wake up the huigitz again, but when I don't hear a cranky roar, I rush over and hug each one of them in turn.

Then, as Tandy, Sierra, and Billie hug each other, I start to back away from everyone else.

"Thank you so much. And I'm so glad you guys are friends again, but now that the huigitz is sleeping… Bye!"

And then I'm off again, with Mal never missing a step to stay beside me.

MALPHAS

Wherever Shannon goes, I will forever follow.

With the faripoz—the flutterbys… no, *butterflies*—continuing to lead us deeper into the shadows, I stay in mine, hovering anxiously just a few steps after my mate. I'm prepared to grab Shannon and tuck her behind the safety of my shadows at any moment. Will she allow it? After the how—despite her fears—she was ready to challenge the huigitz before the other human females calmed the raging beast with their song, I am convinced there is nothing that will ever hold my Shannon back.

I am careful, though. Whoever stole Alana is tricky. Dangerous. It takes a human to think like one of their kind, and though I've spent many cycles in

Shannon's world, there is so much I still do not understand.

Taking someone's spawn? That is not how it is done in Sombra. Nothing will stop me from retrieving her—and I am grateful for the help from my fellow demons and their beloved mates—but, again, it seems as though the shadows and the butterflies are sending us on a wayward path.

I sense Shannon's fear and frustrations traveling down our bond. The only thing I can do is send her another pulse of reassurance.

We will find her. We will get her back.

Shannon stopped running once she realized that the seemingly endless shadows won't welcome such a quick pace. We're in the lead, with Glaine, Billie, and Lucian right behind us. The rest of the human females—Sierra, Hope, Tandy, and Kennedy—are shielded by Sammael, Damien, and Loki, guarding all of our backs. We've formed a circle, our small clan, and it's only after Shannon lets out a sound of anguish as the butterfly flaps its wings before winking into the dark that one of us breaks it.

It's Lucian. The powerful seer steps away from where he was flanking Glaine's mate along with the soldier.

Shannon senses the motion. She turns, eyes accustomed enough to the shadows—and Loki's faint spell —to find Lucian's shape, topped with the vibrant purple mage eyes watching her closely.

My hand reaches for hers, enclosing her trembling fingers in my grasp.

Gratitude and pain hit me, and if I wasn't doing everything a demon possibly could to be strong and brave for his mate, her emotions might have broken me. Just like I thought when she was laboring to give birth to our spawn, I will always do what I can to take her pain from her.

And gratitude? I am her male. I am her *mate*. She never has to thank me for being there to support her.

"Shannon," I murmur.

Twisting her hand in my shadows, she searches for the corporeal form hidden inside of them. Squeezing my finger, as much of my hand as she can hold at the moment, she quiets me before turning her attention to Lucian.

"You've got a roadmap in that head of yours, Lucian. Don't you?"

My Shannon has always had a unique way of putting things. Even though most of the human females have fallen into the habit of speaking in Sombran while they live in Nuit, she uses mortal words and manners of speech regardless of the language. It's something else I adore about her, and if Lucian cocks his head slightly, I'm sure he knows what she means.

Just in case, she huffs and explains. Tapping her temple, she says, "In here. You see where we're going. What we're supposed to do. Like with that huiglwhats-it. You could tell that Billie, Sierra, and Tandy would need to sing together to get around it. Right?"

Lucian nods. "Yes. So much of the future was red, but when the red moon ended, the shadows took its place. Now that we're here… I get flashes. My brother… he *feels*. Even our dear one can tell from our essence that this is it. The beginning of the end."

From her place behind us, Tandy agrees. "He's right, Shannon. Trust me. Whatever Lucian's got in his head, you don't want to see it. You don't want to know what might happen if the rain doesn't stop."

"And the rain won't stop until the baby's tears have dried," murmurs Damien in his soft, sad, lyrical voice.

Shannon's breath hitches. I circle her wrist, tugging gently, tucking her in my arms, murmuring platitudes I only hope are true.

She shudders, her wee human hand a brand against my chest as she needs contact with me.

Lucian takes pity on us. "We doppelseers see not how this will end, only that the path to your child is a winding one."

"No shit. We were going in circles until Freya and the other ungez helped us. Then there was the big moose-lion-looking monster. What the hell is stopping us now?"

Instead of answering Shannon, Lucian glances back at the others. "Ashbalm flower. We need to find an ashbalm flower."

"What's that?"

Shannon is just as confused as I am. An artist all my life, I've rarely approached the edges of Sombra's shadows, let alone gone this far into its depths. I thought I knew every type of flower that could grow among the ash fields of Nuit, but I've never heard of this one.

The dark-haired human female—Sammael's mate—lifts her pale hand. "I know."

"Hope?" My mate doesn't hide her surprise. "You do? What is it?"

Her gaze darts over to Sammael before she gestures around her. "It's a flower. I mean, obviously. But it grows in here. In the shadows." Dropping her hand to her side, she adds, "I had to look for one once."

Sammael's purple eyes flicker. "Haures never should've sent you to search for the flower on your own."

"I wasn't on my own. Loki was with me… for some of it, at least. Besides, none of that matters. The duke was testing me—"

Billie snorts, a sound that reminds me of the Earth pig. "He likes to do that. Prick."

My mate agrees with the assessment that Duke Haures acts like a cock sometimes.

"No argument here," she tells the other women, "but what about the flower? Did you find one? What does it do?"

Hope purses her lips. "Oh, I found it. Loki had to wait outside the shadows, and the duke told me to stick to the edges, but if you follow your nose… you can find the flower."

"Follow your nose? What the hell does that mean?"

"I didn't get it myself at first. But the flower… it calls to you. Like, for me, I smelled the chocolate chip cookies my mom made every Christmas. I followed it, and that's where I found the flower."

I know the delectable scent of a chocolate chip cookie. My Shannon favors them, and though I turned them to ash the first time I attempted to bake them for her in our apartment, I'm proud that I had mastered making them for her while she carried our spawn.

I breathe in deep. "I do not smell any cookies," I say, regret heavy in my tone.

"Me, neither," echoes Sierra.

"Nope," adds Kennedy. "Just the same old mutated rotten eggs stink I remember from this place. No cookies, and believe me… I could go for one about now."

"The ashbalm flower called to Hope so she smelled her mother's treats," says Lucian. "But while she can help you find the flower, the one we seek now is not meant for Sammael's mate. It's meant for yours, Malphas."

"Me?" chirps Shannon. "Why do I need to find this flower? What is it supposed to do anyway?"

"Uh…"

"Hope? What am I missing?"

The dark-haired human worries her bottom lip with her tiny teeth. "The duke said it was necessary to break a mate bond."

My heart leaps up into my throat.

Shannon's fingers dig into my flesh. "I'm not giving up Mal. He's mine."

I'm desperate to rescue Alana. It never occurred to me that I could truly lose my mate as well, and while my worry is barely tempered by her claim, I'd be lying if I said it didn't touch me deep inside that my mate… my love… my flower still *does* claim me.

Just like she did during our first gold moon together, when Glaine and Sammael were sent to put me in enchanted chains and bring me back to Sombra, Shannon announces to everyone gathered that I am her mate.

In the light, I am hers. In the shadows, I am hers.

I strive to be a good male. An honorable male. I like to think that I am, but there isn't anything I won't do to keep her. Same for putting Alana back where she belongs: in her mother's arms—

"It's not for the mate bond you share with the artist," murmurs Damien. "It's for the spawn. The shadows stole her for one reason. To get her back, we must be prepared to break it. You are her mother. She can't retrieve the ashbalm flower. You can."

"Wait." Shannon releases me, and though I miss her touch as she moves away to confront Damien, I let her go. "Someone took my baby. Are you telling me they took her because… no. Break a bond? No way. She's not gonna be mated to *that* kind of monster. She's a *baby*."

Oh, my clever, clever mate. She understood what I'm only just getting now myself. Of course that would explain why someone took Alana from her crib. No one in Sombra will steal a child, but if they believe that child is their one true mate? To guard them, to keep them safe, to watch over them until they're mature enough to accept the mate bond… that has been done in our history.

But not my daughter. Not my Alana.

"There is a bond," begins Lucian.

"Well, there won't be when I'm fucking done. Okay. I've gotta find this flower?" Shannon sniffs the air. Her eyes go wide. "Hang on. Either I'm losing it, or I just got a whiff of coffee."

My Shannon loves coffee. In Sombra, I've introduced her to javits, and she enjoys the buzz she gets from our brewed drink, but she does admit it's not quite the same. So if she's scenting the strong, bitter aroma of human coffee—and the doppelseer is right —it could only be a sign that the ashbalm flower is near.

"Where, my mate?" I ask.

She points. "I think it came from there."

"I'll go with you," offers Hope. "I know what it looks like."

I join the two females. The others stay back at Lucian's urging. He tells Shannon that the ashbalm flower is delicate, both before, during, and after it's been picked from the ash. Hope confirms it, remembering how half of her flower fell apart in her hand.

Shannon is determined. I'm careful to watch the glowing white eyes of the prey and predatory beasts who watch us back, possibly wondering why our clan has split up. If anyone tries to attack my mate and Sammael's, I will throw my body between them to allow them to get the ashbalm flower, then to get away.

Thankfully, that's not necessary. Within minutes, Shannon announces that it's definitely her favorite latte from The Beanery that she's smelling. I don't catch it myself, but it doesn't matter. Her nose led us to it, after all.

It's Hope who sees the flower first, catching Shannon's attention by snagging her arm and pointing down.

The ashbalm flower is about as long as my hand, from wrist to the tip of my claws. Composed of shadows and ash, the bloom is a dancing flame that dims as Shannon crouches down next to him.

"Careful," Hope murmurs. "I plucked it too hard

and lost the whole bottom part of the stem. Sure, I didn't need it because I wasn't giving up Sammael, either, but the duke didn't tell me why I was going after it when he first sent me into the edge of the shadows."

"Maybe you didn't need it," muses Shannon, eyeing the flower closely. "Maybe you just needed to know how to find it."

Hope makes a thoughtful sound. "You mean, like, one day I'd have to tell you how to find it to save Sombra?"

"To save Alana."

"Isn't that the same thing?"

"No," Shannon says firmly. There's no explanation other than that, but there's none needed. Duke Haures… the doppelseers… they want to defeat the prophecy. They want to see Sombra survive.

But my mate? She just wants our daughter back—and so do I.

Without another word, Shannon grips the stem by its base. She gasps as the flame goes out—even though Hope warned her that would happen—before letting out a sigh of relief when only a small part of the stem becomes ash on her fingertips.

Rising up, my mate searches the shadows for me. "Mal, baby. Come here."

I'm there.

Shannon jerks her chin at me. "Hold out your hands."

I do.

Cupping my hands together, creating a valley between them, I'm motionless as Shannon lays the ashbalm flower against my shadows.

"There. I don't have time to coddle that thing. But Mal is made of shadows, too. We can get back to running if we have to, and he'll keep the flower in one piece to break whatever bond some dickhead kidnapper thinks he has with our girl."

My clever, clever mate.

"You ready?" she asks me.

I will guard the ashbalm flower with everything I am. It's only the second most precious one I've ever had the fortune to touch—Shannon's sunflower being the first—but at the moment? It is *everything*.

"Yes, my mate."

"Good. Then let's go."

SHANNON

I wish I could say it was as easy as darting around the slumbering—and *massive*, can't forget that part—huigitz, picking up the human kidnapper's suddenly more frantic boot prints, and because he was flagging after keeping ahead of us for so long… and probably scared shitless of that beast… we found him and Alana is safe and sound.

That's not what happens. Oh, I get around the huigitz with Mal, sending a silent thank you back to the other girls for using their song to put it to sleep because, yeah, that fucker was *huge*. Once Dagon catches up, he finds another slapdash boot print, then points us in the right direction.

With Loki's orb guiding the way, we follow it, but there's still no sign of him or Alana. I strain, listening for my daughter's coos, hearing nothing but a few stray shadow animal noises. The white pinpricks of watching eyes have become few and far between. Mainly because we're so far into the shadows now, if we find one, it'll be a big threat, just like the huigitz.

I'm still determined. My adrenaline is long gone, and part of me wants to slump down to the ash, drop my head into my hands, and sob. Only knowing that Alana needs us—needs *me*—keeps me going. Without a word of complaint, everyone follows.

Well, except for when Hope helped me find the ashbalm flower with Mal. The others hung back, waiting for use to return with it. Lucian nodded in approval after Mal opened his hands just wide enough to show the fragile flower before we were all off again.

That was a half an hour ago at least. Suddenly, a sense of anticipation falls over the shadows. We all feel it. Damien murmurs that it's the end of the beginning, whatever that means, but I only hope that this is the end of the *end*.

Just in case we *are* getting close, our group is quiet. We don't want to let anyone lurking nearby to know that, whatever's been thrown at us, we've gotten past it. Though, I do wonder if my friends have figured out what it took me way too long to see…

As I glance behind me, I realize that Fate brought us all together for a reason.

I grin, my first one since the red moon.

Smart bitch.

Lucian, too. He saw that each of us would have a purpose for coming along on this search. Freya wouldn't have braved the shadows if it wasn't for Kennedy. Hope was with me when we went after the ashbalm. Tandy, Sierra, and Billie were essential to getting past the huigitz.

The prophecy about whether to save Sombra or see its fires extinguished… it's almost like, in a way, all of our destinies brought us to this point. Kennedy wouldn't have been in the shadows, or given Freya if she hadn't bonded with Loki. Hope wouldn't have gone after the ashbalm flower if she wasn't trying to save her bond with Sammael.

Dagon helped Sierra get over her bastard of a cheating ex. Glaine lets Billie take center stage—and helped her with her own journey through the shadows. And Tandy… she finally found someone to love her, even if it happened to be *two* someones with the gift of sight.

And because each one of them found their happily-ever-after, they're here with me, ensuring that mine and Mal's gets to continue.

We just need our baby back, and as the air in the shadows starts to stir—the first gust of something that might be wind rushing past us—I can't help but hope that this… this is it. We've done it.

Up ahead, there's another block. I've become an expert at spotting them. As dark as it is in here, the wards are even darker. They are imposing. Threatening. They warn us from moving on, but when we find a way past them, they reluctantly let us go.

This one? It's the largest one we've encountered. It spreads as far as I can see, and I don't have much hope of getting around it if this isn't the sort of block that we can climb under. It reminds me of the final boss level in a video game. That we've done every challenge we've had to, and if we can just confront who is hiding behind the shadows, I'll finally find my daughter.

Only one problem.

Before I can even attempt to approach it, a white ball appears between us. It starts small, the size of a golf ball maybe, before it grows and it grows and, holy shit, it's now bigger than a hula hoop.

It's super bright, too. It doesn't lose the white color, and as it gleams against the dark shadow background, it freaking glows so much, my eyes burn.

I know what it is, though. It might not be like any one I've ever seen—considering portals from Earth to Sombra look more like flames than an eclipse—but that?

That's a portal.

I glance at Sammael. "I thought you can't create a shadow portal in here."

Sammael frowns. "I cannot. And that is my specialty. If I can't do it, it cannot be done."

Loki grunts softly. "It is taking all of my magic just

to keep the orb spell running. The shadows suck it in faster than I can create it."

"No need now," says Billie pointedly. "Whatever's happening, we're all gonna sear our retinas by the time it's done."

She's not wrong. At least for the human women, we've gotten used to the darkness inside of the shadows. Loki's spell saved us from walking into the trees or tripping over the bones, but it's still like walking around the woods at night with only the moon above to help us see.

That large white circle? Whatever it is, it's not a shadow portal. Not really. And it's not anything like the summoning spell that yanked Mal out of Sombra and into my apartment.

Still, even as I squint so that it doesn't completely blind me, I can't help but watch its glow get impossibly brighter.

Mal drapes his arm over my shoulder, tugging me close in an adorably protective manner. Like he's prepared to battle whoever— or whatever—might pop out of that light…

A moment later, we're about to find out because four notable silhouettes appear in the distance. They're linked, holding hands as they zoom toward us, and it's easy to tell from the sizes that the figures on the ends are demon males, with the two in the center definitely human women.

Together, they step out of the portal. The white

light blinks out from behind them. It takes me a few seconds to make sure my eyes are still working right before I look up at them and see—

"Your Grace," breathes out Sammael, reverence in his tone. "I did not know that you possessed travel magic."

Duke Haures is on the left. Holding his hand, I see a pretty brunette with a vaguely familiar face. She's dressed in a gorgeous blue dress, her hair piled up on top of her head. Amy Benoit—my friend from Connecticut—is holding onto her, though she releases the other woman once the portal thing disappears. And, since Amy's here, the identity of the second male becomes obvious: Nox, Amy's Sombra demon mate.

Duke Haures's pale skin glows just as brightly as his portal did beneath the sliver of the Sombra moon. He shakes his head royally, the light from Loki's orb spell winking off of his crystal crown.

"I do not need travel magic," he tells his former mage haughtily. "I am Sombra's ruler. More than that, I am a bondmaster. My essence belongs to my mate, but I share a bond with every one of my people. Once Lucian summoned me to tell me it was time, the duchess and I have answered his call."

Wow. All this time, I thought people were, like, sending him the Sombra version of a letter. Or a magical email. But he has bonds with all of his people?

Well, *that's* terrifying.

And duchess… no wonder I thought the woman clinging to him looked vaguely familiar. She looks similar enough to Amy that they could be sisters—or an aunt and her niece.

Dagon nods a greeting to the brunette clutching Haures's arm.

She smiles warmly at him. "It's good to see you again, Dagon."

Sierra grabs her demon's arm. "Hello, Susanna. Remember me?"

Her laugh is soft and sweet. "Of course, Sierra. Congratulations on the baby. I'm so glad the time has come that we don't have to be afraid of the gold moon. That Alana is only the first of a new generation of Sombrans."

Alana… she knows about my baby. I mean, duh. Of course she knows about my baby. I tell Mal everything, and now that he knows better than to try to protect me again, he does the same for me. Why wouldn't the duke go home and tell his mate about the half-human, half-demon child that might lead to the end of the world he rules?

As if she knows what I'm thinking, she turns to me. "Shannon. It's so good to finally meet you. Don't worry. I got us into this. I'm going to get us out."

Uh… what?

Before I can ask, Amy catches my attention. "Hey. Don't worry. We got this."

She sounds so sure, I want to believe her. And then I think: why not?

Just like the rest of us, maybe Lucian saw something that includes them. He's the one who summoned Haures. If he needed the duke, I honestly believe that the duke would never take his mate out of the safety of the capital unless the doppelseer saw her with him. Amy, too. Nox is a fierce hunter, even if he lives in the human world. He wouldn't take a trip to Sombra, then join Amy and the others in the shadows unless *he* had to.

Maybe because Haures threatened him with another stint in the dungeons… fourteen years were enough for the scowly, red-eyed hunter, I'm sure, and other than nodding at the other demons, he stays quiet.

I scoff, more amazed than anything else at this moment.

Fucking Fate.

You know, I thought something was up when Sierra and Hope visited Nuit at the same time that Billie was home, Kennedy was usually there, and even Tandy came along with her mates. I know Susanna is always in Mavro. That meant we were only missing Amy… but something tells me she was here, too.

Is that what the gods were waiting for? Did we all have to be in Sombra to watch as the prophecy that began with Alana's birth happen?

Again, I think about my earlier realization.

Kennedy knows about life in the shadows, plus she has a pet ungez that saved the freaking day by helping us find a way around the block. Sierra, Billie, and Tandy needed to use their three-part harmony to quiet a savage shadow beast. Hope was a huge help when it came to finding the ashbalm.

We're all here for a reason.

What about Amy and Susanna?

I have no doubt in my mind that the gods needed them here. Add that to Susanna's comment about her getting 'us' into this mess…

"Susanna?"

Okay. Maybe I put a little too much accusation into her name because Haures bares his tusks at me, his vibrant blue eyes flaring in warning.

Right. I gentle my tone. "What are you…" Hm. How do I put this nicely? I try again. "Why are you all here?"

Susanna doesn't look offended, even if her mate does. However, she doesn't get the chance to answer before Lucian speaks up.

"Susanna is the only one who has ever faced Yelios. Five decades have passed. It is finally time that she ends what began so long ago… I've seen it. I didn't know what it meant then, though I understand now. Alana is the child of prophecy, but it began with Susanna."

Okay. First things first—

The name sounds familiar, but… "Who the hell is Yelios?"

At the same time as Mal says, "the former king," and Sammael tells us, "Queen Alana's mate," and Glaine says, "a fierce soldier," Damien's eyes brighten until they're closer to lavender than dark purple.

It's his voice that carries over all the others as he gestures around him. "*This* is Yelios."

"The shadows were the deposed king's home," adds Lucian.

King. Wait. I know this story. Mal told me about the bravest demon queen in their history, and the king who tried to avenge her for centuries before he seemingly walked into the shadows one day and Haures took his throne…

Tandy gasps, covering her mouth with her fingers. "But now he *is* the shadows." She shakes her head, her voice returning to normal instead of continuing to take on her mates' prophesying tones. "Oh, gross. We've spent hours crawling around inside of some ancient, crazed king."

Oh, I hope she's wrong. I really, really do because, suddenly, I have a sinking feeling in my stomach about why we had to journey as far as we did to get to this point and we *still* haven't seen a sign of my daughter.

The sinking suspicion only drops lower when Haures says, "Apollyon tells me that it was a human male who stole the spawn. I suspected this might happen one day, and Lucian's recent visions only confirmed it. But, fear not, Malphas. Shannon. It's not the human who sought your child. He only took her to deliver her to Yelios. And Yelios will never harm her which means that the human won't either."

To be fair, that does make me feel the teensiest bit better. As much as I fucking *hate* the idea that somebody broke into my house, kidnapped my baby, and decided to hide her in the shadows, I have the tiniest amount of relief to hear that she's at least safe.

But it's only a small amount because it just doesn't make sense to me.

"Why would he want her? I mean, what kind of monster kidnaps a *baby*?"

Nox clears his throat. "My mate was a spawn of only eight human years when I first recognized that Amy was meant to be mine."

Though I already knew the story of their mating, I'm not surprised that Amy tugs on his arm before saying, "Not helping, hon."

He shrugs, unrepentant. "I waited until you were a mature female," he reminds her. "No honorable Sombran would ever claim a child."

Hang on—

"Alana is not his mate," I argue. "She's a baby, remember?" When no one rushes to tell me that I'm right, not even Malphas, I turn to Lucian. "Okay." So the human guy didn't take Alana for himself. He took him for Yelios. That's still a *hell*, no. "Tell me that my baby isn't fated to be mated to *that* monster."

"No," says Lucian. "Your Alana has a far greater destiny. If we can save Sombra, she will go on to save Noctavara."

Save *what?*

"Her path is to save Sombra, but never stay, her fate tied to the one with a shadow for a heart, a gilded touch, and the wrong way," intones Damien. "For her broken wings will only end the curse when her own heart stops."

This is not the time for another one of his prophecies, even if it suggests that Alana will survive today. *Today.* Because the rest of what Damien said…

Heart stops.

Stops?

Stops?

"But Alana is immortal."

"She has human blood." Haures. God damn it, why does the duke have to sound so *smarmy* right now? "It will be a lot easier for her to be killed because of that."

I fist my hands. "Do you think you might not tell me how fragile my daughter is when some insane demon king has her?" I shake my head. "And why would he take her in the first place? He had a mate. Queen—"

Oh, *fuck.*

Malphas is right there, supporting me as I start to fall. "No. It's just a name. Mal wanted to name her after a strong demoness. She's not the real Alana. She's *our* Alana."

"I did," my mate agrees. "To honor the fallen queen, and to show that she could grow to be a fierce warrior."

"You couldn't have known," cuts in Susanna. "You couldn't have known that Yelios has spent ages waiting for his mate to return to him."

Come again?

Suddenly, the air crackles. It sounds like something's being rent apart, torn, *broken*. It rips, echoes, and though nothing looks different at all, the wind rushes past again, sending my ponytail whipping around my face.

Kennedy stumbles. Loki catches her.

Malphas crouches down at my side, hands folding over to protect the ashbalm flower in his hold.

Amy turns into Nox's chest. He goes from a solid demon like Haures to shadows like the others, though I know it's not on purpose. Nox lost control of his shadows long ago when he sacrificed most of his essence to escape the dungeon Haures put him in so he could save Amy from her human ex in the mortal world. The wind must have triggered his switch, though that does nothing to stop him from shielding Amy from the wind.

But Susanna… she stands tall and proud as she shifts on her heels, facing the wind.

"Yelios. Can you hear me? I know you can. And I know what you've done."

In response, a voice that sounds like it belongs to someone who's lived for two thousand years and smoked a pack a day for each and every one of them calls out, so loudly I feel the rasp all the way down to my bones.

Holy shit. Tandy wasn't kidding. The voice comes from all around us, and there is no doubt in my mind that it's coming from the shadows.

Coming from King Yelios.

"Ah… so at last you return to me, Susanna. You did not bring the child to me as you vowed, but I am a merciful king. I have my mate. I consider our bargain complete. I have that which is important to me. And now… I return to you what I took."

He spoke in Sombran. His voice is so aged, it takes me a second to understand what he—Yelios—said to the duke's mate.

A second is all it takes for the large block in front of us to crack open enough to spit out a body before it crumples on the ash.

A human male-sized body that groans before flopping to his back.

CHAPTER 19
REVELATIONS

SHANNON

That's not Alana.

That's all I care about. It's not Alana, and because it isn't, I couldn't care less what the identity of the human who took her from her crib is. He's dead, that's what he is, whether Yelios killed him or I'm about to. But, to me, he's just some guy.

But not to Susanna and Amy.

"Daniel? Dan? Is that you?"

"Dad? Oh my god. Dad!"

Target.

He should be dead. However, no one is making a move toward the man except for Amy and Susanna, who drop down at his side—and they're obviously not going to kill him. Shit. Sammael might not be able to conjure a shadow portal in here, but what about chains?

No? Oh, well. That's okay.

Let this human chick handle it.

"Hey, if you're not about to get on with the stabby-stabby," I snap, Glaine's heavy sword suddenly in my grasp, "then *I* will."

It was easier than I expected it to be to steal it. To duck under Mal's hold, dash over to Glaine, and snatch the damn sword. The only reason I even could was because—like the rest of us—the practiced soldier is too stunned to realize that Yelios has been working with a human to stop me. Because, no matter what, one thing is clear: Amy's father... Susanna's brother-in-law... is the man who took my baby to give to the shadows.

But he's not a mate, so that means his ass is *mine*.

"Duke's first law," I remind us all. Not like we haven't heard the endless refrain over the years, but I say it anyway: "Humans can't know about Sombra unless they're a mate. Something tells me that, if this prick stole my baby to give to another asshole, they're not bonded. So he dies, right?"

Fuck the first law. I could give a shit, but I'm so *furious* right now that I'd happily swing this heavy-ass sword and lop off his head if only to make him pay for ever laying his kidnapping human fingers on Alana.

No one comes between a mama bear and her cub.

No one, except a daughter who has been estranged from her father since she was a little girl, even if she didn't understandnwhy.

A daughter who might finally, finally get a little bit of closure as she holds onto the man who, like Amy, hasn't aged a day since he got involved with Sombra demons.

Only… Amy is Nox's mate. He gifted her with his immortality when he gave her his essence and bonded her to him.

Daniel Benoit... and, okay, that's not his name since I know Amy changed her name to her mother's maiden name and that's why it matches her maternal aunt… but until I know what name is going on his tombstone, Benoit will do… he should be at least mid-sixties, early-seventies based on Amy's age. Tired, covered in dust, and broken, he still doesn't look a day over forty himself.

But why?

And does it really matter when *he kidnapped Alana*?

I take a step toward him, holding the sword.

"Shannon, please."

Amy.

Amy, the woman who received a frantic message on an old social media platform and actually answered it. Amy, the woman who has only ever been a phone call or a short drive away when I needed to talk to someone who knew what it was like to be a Sombra demon's mate.

Amy, my friend for the last two-plus years.

Damn it.

"Oh, fine." Turning, I shove the sword back at Glaine. The scowling demon tightens his grip, as though girding himself against a tiny blonde human 2/3rds his size snatching it from him again. "But he better have a good explanation."

"I can explain." Susanna rises, leaving Amy to help pull her father up into a seated position. "When I first was pulled into Sombra, my mate sent me into the shadows to find an ashbalm flower."

Haures sets his jaw. "I gave you a choice to break your bond. You didn't want to stay at first."

"You put me in the dungeon."

"To keep you safe, my love."

"To keep me, you mean," Susanna counters. "And you knew I wouldn't use the ashbalm, just like Hope didn't when you gave her the same choice."

Haures cocks his head, conceding her point.

"Anyway," Susanna continues, "I went into the shadows. I… I got lost. Instead of finding the ashbalm, I found Dagon. The shadows were killing him." She pauses a moment. "Yelios was killing him."

As if I had any illusions that the king can't hear us or doesn't know everything that is going on in his shadows, he makes sure to cut in and rasp out, "This part of Sombra is still my domain. I am still king here. If you do not bow, you do not survive."

Sierra grabs her mate's arm. "Dagon?"

"I am loyal to Duke Haures," he explains. "I bow to no other ruler. Now, I get on my knees for none but you, Sierra, but Yelios… Susanna saved my life that day."

"Because I'm human. Because a seer told Yelios after his Alana died that she would be returned to him, a demon child with a human mother."

Like *my* Alana.

Oh, no.

"I'm human. That intrigued him. So when I told him to let Dagon go, he agreed as long as I promised to give him my firstborn child. A child of a human mother and a demon father… the child that Lucian and Damien saw in their visions two thousand years before I was even born."

But Susanna and Haures never had children. I always thought that was odd. I mean, fifty years worth of gold moons and they never had an oopsie? Unless… unless Haures knew of a prophecy about the first demon-human halfling—and his mate promised away her firstborn child.

Her firstborn, not *mine*.

"I said what I had to to escape." Susanna sighs, trembling slightly. "But I didn't know then that a vow in Sombra… you can't break it. He gave me Dagon's life. Since I didn't have a child yet and possibly never would, he said he would take something I hold dear until I complete our bargain."

She pauses, waiting to see if Yelios will interject again. When he doesn't, she glances down at the human man who is now sitting up, leaning against Amy, his eyes drawn to the ash, both dazed and obviously ashamed.

He doesn't say a word, either.

"I didn't know it was Dan," she says, voice gone soft. "I don't even know how he got involved. I haven't seen him since 1987… but that's Dan. Mindy's husband… that's Amelia's father."

"Dad," Amy ruffles the back of his dark blond head. "I… you left Mom. You left us. What happened?"

"I, too, want to hear it from the human," announces Haures.

I'm with both of them.

"I transferred essence from a demon who came to escape his existence in my shadows," Yelios rumbles instead when it becomes clear that the man won't just yet. "I tied Daniel to me so that he could do my bidding."

Technically, that's possible. Sombra demons usually wait until they've found their one true mate to initiate the essence exchange because they can only have one. You have to be absolutely sure that the lover you picked is the one you want to spend forever with before you do the exchange, and if they don't give you their essence back, you're screwed.

So if Yelios made another demon give their essence to Daniel Benoit, I wouldn't have been surprised if it drove him nuts. That, plus it would explain why he's in Sombra now—though I guess that means his head's not on the chopping block at the moment—and why he looks so young.

But why—

"The book," blurts out Amy's father. His voice is rusty, unused, and there is pure grief in the sound. "He made me send the book where it needed to go. To constantly remind me, year after year, that I wouldn't be free until he had what he wanted."

Yelios's harsh laugh sends shivers down my spine. "The doppelseers see much, but they don't see everything. I knew that the firstborn halfling would be my Alana returned to me. I made it so that every gods-given mated pair found each other so that I found *her* again."

I'm not dumb enough to point out that he could've stopped after I hooked up with Mal. If he had, the book never would've made it to Hope or Sierra. The others… since Kennedy took the book from me, and both Billie and Tandy could've read it since Sierra kept it after she found Dagon… but still. As for me… maybe that explains how the *Grimoire du Sombra* found its way to Turn the Page in the first place…

"It's my fault," the man says. His voice is thick, tears streaming down his ragged, stubble-covered cheeks. "All I did was look for the book that Su was obsessed with. I thought it might be worth a couple of bucks. I had a wife. A little girl. Su took off, leaving everything behind. How was I supposed to know that it was a demon spellbook? Or that, when he caught me with it, he'd drag me through a portal to Hell?"

Not Hell, but I get the point.

Daniel Benoit gulps. "I told him Su was my sister-in-law. My family. And he told me that day I was his until Su gave him what he wanted. But Su didn't. And I… oh, *Amy*… I had to take the baby. You see that, right?" Glassy eyes lock on my friend. "I lost mine. But to get her back… to get my sweet Amy back… he wanted his mate. His eyes… they were green. Do you see them, sweetheart?"

Amy pats his head, eyes wild and confused as she searches for Nox.

Me?

I've had enough.

"He's not her mate!"

"Shannon, my flower—"

"He's not, Mal. You know it. *I* know it—"

"And so I do," says Haures. "I am the bondmaster. Whatever Yelios says, his bond died when Queen Alana did. She had all the essence he had to give. He can't give anymore. I vow it. He is not the spawn's mate."

"No," agrees Lucian. "I see her mate, and—"

As long as it's not Yelios, I can deal with that later. Especially since that other prophecy said Alana's heart might stop once she finds her one true mate. But since that's a *later* problem, and this is a *now* problem…

"His eyes were green," mumbles Dan. "But they're white now."

"He is lost," adds Loki. "There is no reaching him."

"And he has my daughter?"

"He believes she is his queen." That's Dan again. Now that he's spoken up, it's like he thinks if he keeps going, if he helps, I might not reach for Glaine's sword again. "He will keep her until she is old enough to bond with him. But he was afraid he'd lose Alana again… that's why he had me take her."

He did that because he's *insane.*

"There is no bond," Haures repeats.

I really fucking hope the bondmaster is right.

"Of course there is," comes Yelios's thunderous reply. Because, yup, he's still spying on us. "How else could I beckon the red moon?"

Hang on—

He did that?

"Impossible," snaps Haures. "You were never a mage. You were a soldier—"

"It is my gift. Just like you have yours, Haures. To

share the love I have for my mate with the rest of her people."

This is insane. Like… I can't be the only one thinking that this is insane.

"She's a *baby*," I howl.

Malphas knows me. Words are never just enough, and I've done everything I could to hold back while all of this was being dumped on us. But I can't anymore. I don't care that these shadows *are* Yelios. He has her somewhere, and if he opened up the wall to spit Daniel out, there's got to be a way for me to get to Alana now.

I played nice.

I'm done playing.

I don't know what the odds are that Glaine will be caught off-guard enough for me to snatch his sword again. I don't know if it's powerful enough to cut through shadows, or to kill a king that his people thought died two thousand years ago. Glaine didn't try to cut them before because, like any rational people, we thought the shadows were just freaking shadows.

But they're not, and if he exists at all with a corporeal form—and he has to, right, if he could slip into the human world to steal Daniel—then I can stab him.

Right?

Won't hurt to try. And, before anyone can stop me, I finally make a break for it.

I don't make it two steps until Malphas is in front of me, one arm cradling my head, the other wrapped around my back, pulling me up against his shadowy chest as he stops me dead in my tracks.

Damn it. Malphas *really* knows me.

I wiggle. "Let me go, Mal. Our baby needs us."

"I know, my Shannon. But think about this. The shadows feed on all who enter them. It's not just the predators we have to fear. They take everything we are until all that's left is despair. And then we're gone. Lost. He pulls us into him. He hasn't let that happen yet, but I have no doubt that he will." Mal nuzzles the top of my head with his chin, warm breath fanning my hair. "I will not lose you, Shannon."

"He has her, Mal. He has Alana."

"I know." He presses a kiss to my hair. "And if Haures won't end this, I will."

What?

"Nox?"

"Yes, Malphas?"

"Guard my Shannon for me."

The air shifts. "Of course."

It happens so damn fast. One second, I'm clinging to my mate. The next? He's carefully, gently, *quickly* passing me over to Amy's. The imposing hunter accepts my trembling body with a solemn nod, my back tucked into his side, a giant shadowy hand pinning me next to him.

That's what that slight breeze was from. He

zipped from where he was with Amy over to me as soon as my mate asked him to. He's strong in his shadows, so strong I can't break free of his hold, and when he winks back to his solid form, it's *impossible* to escape him.

I watch as Malphas stands up, straight-backed and brave, the hunter inside of my gentle artist coming out as he moves toward the wall of shadows. Toward Yelios. He doesn't run, like I had. He doesn't glance back or even think to grab Glaine's sword.

It's just Malphas, hair swaying down his back, sculpted shadow arms starting to glow with the echoes of the golden runes that first appeared when I summoned him so many years ago.

"Yelios," he calls, his voice careful yet strong. "Do you hear me? I am Alana's father. You think she is your one true mate? Then answer me!"

"Malphas," is Yelios's sneer of a response.

Shit. I shouldn't be surprised that he knows my mate's name. If he *is* the shadows, he probably knows everything about us.

The fucker is toying with us!

I hiss, but Mal stares into the wall. "Tell me of your bond. Not the one you have with Queen Alana. But my spawn… does she make your heart skip a beat? Do your claws ache to touch her pretty yellow hair? When she peers up at you, do you know that there isn't anything in any world that you won't do to see her smile?"

My mate is asking Yelios about Alana, but the examples he uses… he's talking about me.

Despite all of the other emotions rushing through me—fear and despair and anger and that sliver of hope—my heart swells. Mal… god, I fucking love him.

He doesn't want to lose me. Well, I don't want to lose him, either.

Especially when he lifts his voice and says solemnly, "Does she amaze you every single moment that you're lucky to be by her side?"

"My Alana did," Yelios confesses, his answer carrying away on a renewed breeze. "And when I have a bond with the one returned to me, she someday will, too."

When I have a bond…

Because there *is* no bond.

"The seer was wrong," Haures announces. "Alana cannot be returned to you, Yelios. But I can set you free so you can return to her."

The duke clicks his claws together. "Malphas. The ashbalm flower."

It takes a moment for Mal to tear his gaze away from the shadows. I'm watching the same thing he is, and in the depths, I see a pair of white eyes—the size and shape and height revealing they could belong to a Sombra demon—staring back at him. But once Haures clicks his claws again, the spell is seemingly broken. Mal jerks his head, giving Yelios his back, before gliding over to Haures.

His right hand is still cupped, cradling the ashbalm flower.

My whole body thrums with anticipation.

I'd given up on thinking the ashbalm would do anything as soon as Haures first mentioned that, as a bondmaster, he could tell that there was none between my Alana and the warped king. But Mal… all this time, my demon mate guarded it with everything he had. Even as he grabbed me, held me close, tucked me against him… he never once dropped it or smashed it.

And now he offers it to Haures.

I don't understand. "If he doesn't have a bond with Alana, what do you need that for?"

"It's not for his imagined bond with your spawn. It's for the bond he had with his queen that he's let become twisted over the last two thousand years."

He holds his white hand over the ashbalm flower nestled securely in Malphas's palm.

Haures's blue eyes gleam as he addresses the shadows. "I release you. Go, Yelios. Go to where the shadows beckon you, and your one true mate has spent ages waiting for you to return to her."

The ashbalm flower bursts into flame. Malphas doesn't remove his hand until the fire dies and the ashbalm flower is simply ash once more.

I wait with bated breath. Behind me, none of the others make a sound until—

A single gasp before the ancient voice croaks out one name: "*Alana.*"

Please, please, please let this work.

I watch the white eyes in the shadows. To my surprise, I see a flash of green eyes, just like Daniel Benoit said, and then… *nothing.*

One.

Two.

Three.

It would probably be more accurate to call the rush of wind that explodes from the wall of shadows a tornado. It bursts out powerfully, slamming into all of us. My hair flies around my face, the ash eddying up into my eyes, my nose, my mouth. Mal rushes over, trying to shield me. I cling to him and only hope that everyone else is clutching their own seven-foot-tall demon.

When the wind dies, I blink as much ash out of my eyes as possible before checking to see if my friends are okay. It's easy to do that because, suddenly, the shadows disperse. All of them. The wall, the heavy, weighted blackness around us… it's still dark in here, but closer to what the shadows gathering around the back of Nuit look like rather than the nearly impenetrable ones that serve as a border to the edge of Sombra.

I can see in front of me, and what I notice first, as

though a tug inside of me yanked me in the exact direction to look, is something left behind from when the shadows—*Yelios*—disappeared.

Over the stunned silence left in the gale's wake, another voice calls out that name: "Alana!"

This time, it's mine.

Because there, sitting in the ash, her golden eyes bright, her chubby cheeks pink, her fangs peeking out from her wide, contented smile, with a single glowing butterfly flapping its wings over her head is *our* Alana.

CHAPTER 20
HAPPILY-EVER-AFTER

SHANNON

I have my baby back.

A quick once-over reveals that she's exactly the same as she was when I saw her last. True, that means she needs a diaper change and plenty of milk—and I can finally acknowledge that, damn, my tits *hurt* from not being able to feed her or pump—but apart from that and a little ash on her nose, she's my sweet, happy baby and I will never, ever let her out of my sight again.

As soon as I pronounced her perfect, Mal swooped both of us up in his arms. I pepper kisses to his face next because, damn it, I've never loved anyone as much as I love these two.

Kennedy tiptoes forward, giving Alana a relieved pat. "Welcome back, sweetheart."

We're not back yet. We're a good three or four-hour walk from Nuit, but I don't care about that. I have my baby. The threat to her is gone and—

"The rain has stopped," Lucian announces. His purple eyes shine in the hazy, reddish light surrounding us. "The fires in Sombra still burn. The child… by being the catalyst to release Yelios from his purgatory and make the shadows of Sombra safe again… she has saved us all."

I squeeze her to me. "Not bad for a four-month-old."

"That is not all that the spawn has done," adds Haures, drawing our attention to him. Then, to the shock of every single one of us gathered, the solid pale-skinned duke does something I don't think he ever could: he shifts completely to shadow, the blue eyes shining from his dark face the only clue that he *is* Haures.

With a crook of his claw, he gestures for Susanna to come to him. Moving slowly, a small smile tugging on her lips, she does. Haures gathers her up in his shadows and, without another word, he lifts her up into the sky, then zips away.

In an instant, they're gone, and I know I'm not the only one whose mouth drops open to see them go.

"We just made him even more powerful," I announce to no one in particular.

Somewhere behind me, Billie sighs. "Yup."

Ah, well. Sombra is my home now. Maybe having

a terrifying demon in charge of this realm will only help keep my daughter safe.

As long as he stays in the capital, that is. I'll stick to Nuit, thank you very much. That's where I belong.

Anywhere my mate is, that's where I'll always be…

I snuggle against him. Sammael and Loki are murmuring to each other. So are Tandy and Lucian. Amy looks like she wants to leave her father behind and head over to Nox, but that she also feels bad about abandoning him. Dan is curled up in the fetal position, probably feeling the aftereffects of Yelios leaving Sombra, so… yeah. Totally get that.

Nox is looking up at the sky thoughtfully. For one second, he's in his solid form. He blinks. Shadows. Blinks again. Solid form, and I finally notice that the shadowy bands that always existed around his wrists —a memento of the time he spent in the enchanted gold chains—are *healed*.

Marveling at his hands, he shows them to Amy.

She gasps, her eyes shining with unshed tears. They're happy ones now, and Nox flies over to his mate, embracing her while ignoring the trembling man beside them.

"It's in their blood," Damien says, watching them. "Two women, kin from the same line, both with the gift to mate a broken shadow and make him whole."

Look at that. I guess now I know why Susanna and Amy Benoit were each destined to be a Sombra demon's mate. If I thought it was a big, honking coincidence that the three members of Thr33peat were, it was even weirder that an aunt and her niece were.

But, like Damien said, if it was in their blood…

Hope makes a small sound in the back of her throat. "Sam? I was just thinking… since Yelios was the shadows and he's, you know, gone now? Can you open the portal to Earth? Or do we have to wait until we get back to Nuit?"

It doesn't take a mage to open a portal to Earth. Mal can do it because I summoned him to me with the *verus amor* spell; after, there was a pathway open between his world and mine. Same with every other demon and human mated pair here.

Still, Sammael is the first to try because Hope is the first to realize that that might be possible. He conjures with his hand, a small cheer of triumph erupting from our very exhausted group when a fiery portal appears near him and Hope.

"Oh, I'm so glad. I need a shower and a bed." She motions for him to bend down. He does. She loops her arms around his shoulders, hooking her legs around his waist. "Take me home?"

"Always, Hope."

He nods at the rest of us while Hope waves her goodbye. I don't blame her for cutting out so quickly, and I only, well, *hope* that our trip back to Nuit can be as fast as that.

"Roy knows to check in with Three when I 'go on

vacation'," Sierra says next, doing air quotes. "I didn't expect us to be gone this long after checking with Azazel, but he comes by twice a day to feed him, play with him, and scoop the box, so I'm sure Three's good. But I miss him, so I want to go back, too. You ready, demon?"

While her mate bobs his head in agreement, I cradle Alana to me before rushing over to him. I squeeze his muscular arm. "Thank you, Dagon. For everything… I really mean it."

He bows his head. "Someone saved me in these shadows once before, and I was able to find my one true mate. We will have our spawn soon. Without Susanna, none of this would've been possible. I never could repay her. Instead, I helped you. And, one day, Alana will help someone else. So the circle goes."

Alana is going to be lucky if I don't ask Haures to keep her safe and sound in Mavro once she gets older…

I smile. "Very true. But, still, thanks."

Like Sammael, Dagon opens the portal that will lead back to Sierra's penthouse apartment. Before they step into it, Tandy gets Sierra's promise that they'll meet up again the next time Sierra has to visit Azazel.

Billie points at Sierra. "Boop Three on the nose for me, Sierra."

"You got it, Bee."

And, with that, Sierra and Dagon are gone.

After that, the Sombra gods finally seem to have decided to throw me a bone here because, once our numbers have dwindled a little, Loki tests his magic. Turns out, he's able to create a portal that would bring us right back to the village square of Nuit, saving us all that time traveling back.

Tandy, Lucian, and Damien agree to return with us before heading to their enchanted cabin. Billie and Glaine decide to stay in Nuit a little longer so they're coming, too. Obviously, Loki's leading his mate and her ungez back, and there's no way I'm sticking around here with my baby and Mal.

All I want to do is feed Alana, change her, bathe her, and snuggle on the couch with her and my demon. I'm eager to jump right into Loki's portal, but before I do, Kennedy clears her throat.

"Hey, Amy?" asks Kennedy. "You guys want to come back with us? Or is Nox gonna bring you home?"

Amy and Nox exchange a look before she smiles softly at Kennedy. "Thanks, but we'll be okay. Besides, I think I'm just gonna sit with my dad a little longer."

A guilty twinge ties my stomach up in knots. Now that I have Alana, I kinda feel bad for my murderous turn back there. "If you need anything—"

She nods. "Thanks. And, for what it's worth, I'm glad your baby is okay."

Me, too, Amy. Me, too.

M ALPHAS HOVERS AROUND OUR BABY AND ME THE
entire time I do her normal nighttime routine. We
both figured—after we showed Apollyon and Lilith
that Alana was safe and sound—that moving forward
and acting like it was any old regular night was the
way to go.

I fed her. Mal bathed her. I put her in a new
diaper and a change of clothes, then rocked her in the
cradle until she was asleep.

Then, and only then, did I collapse against Mal.

I stink. I'm sweaty and dirty and there is ash in
parts of me that I wish there wasn't ash. My body
aches. Good chance I have blisters on my blisters
because my stupid ass didn't bother with socks when I
hurried and got dressed all those hours ago.

Do I care? Does Mal as I basically climb into his
lap once we're both sitting in the burnt tree rocking
chair in the corner of the nursery?

Not even a little.

He holds me close, chest rumbling as he says, "I
love you."

"Mm. I love you, too, big guy."

"I worship you, my Shannon. My heart is in your
hands. I never want it anywhere else." He presses a
kiss to my lips. "You amaze me. To see you so forceful,
so fearless… you absolutely amaze me. I am in awe of

everything you do, and if I had lost you? I would've been lost as well."

I nip Mal's bottom lip, then take advantage of the way he gasps to turn his peck into a deep kiss.

Only then, when I feel myself getting light-headed from lack of air and sudden need, do I pull back far enough to gaze into his stunning gold eyes.

"You're never gonna lose me, babe. This is it. The three of us forever… you're stuck with me."

"There is nowhere I'd rather be. In Sombra, Earth… another world… we are together. And we always will be."

"Damn right, Mal. But we're not going anywhere else." I shrug impishly. "Sombra's grown on me."

"Really?"

"Really."

Looking down at the pure devotion etched into his demon features, I grin. God, it feels good to grin.

This is it.

Shannon in Sombra.

Forever.

I helped take down a crazed king. No matter how he looks at it, Haures has my family to thank for his power upgrade and the future of his people. I didn't lop off Amy's dad's head with Glaine's sword, even though that fucker totally deserved it. I helped rescue my baby, leading to the end of the rains.

And this male is amazed by me.

Oh, yeah. I kick ass at being a Sombra demon's mate.

Know what else?

I'm a reader. Always have been, and if there's one thing I know about my favorite type of books, it's that every good romance ends with a happily-ever-after.

Malphas is immortal. Thanks to the essence exchange, so am I. My big, sweet monster promised me forever. I told him I'm holding him to it, and as I cuddle up against him, Alana secure in her cradle on the other side of the room, my heart rate finally back to normal after the frantic, determined journey through the deepest, darkest shadows of Sombra, I finally grin again.

This is it. My HEA.

With an artist I adore. A baby I'll do anything for. A world just waiting for me to leave my mark on it.

I couldn't ask for more.

Do I know what happened to the *Grimoire du Sombra* after Tandy read the true love spell that led her to find Damien and Lucian? No, and I'm pretty sure none of us do. Maybe it's done what it needed to, bringing us all together to keep the doppelseers' prophecy from coming to pass. Maybe some lonely demon will be ripped out of their bathtub, summoned in front of another human woman who will ogle the baseball bat between his thighs before noticing the glowing eyes and pointed horns…

Hey. It happened once before. Thinking back to

the women who helped me save Alana, it's more like it happened *eight* times.

But this one is *my* story, even though I'm sure there will be plenty of adventures to come during our forever. I have my monster mate, and even if I realize now that we might argue, and the villagers might give me odd looks, and Sombra isn't some fantastical fairy world without dangers of its own… fuck, it.

I'm happy.

Ever.

After.

EPILOGUE

ALANA

TWENTY-FIVE YEARS LATER

The butterflies find me everywhere.

For as long as I can remember, the gentle, peaceful creatures enjoy fluttering around my head. When I'm in a playful mood, I bat my hand at them, knowing that they find it a game to dodge my fingers so they can perch on the tiny nub of one of my horns.

I always hoped my dainty horns would grow into something more pointed and as powerful as my father's. Even the demonesses in our village—most of them born in Soleil and moved to Sombra—have long, delicate horns that make them fiercely beautiful.

And then there's me. With my mom's colorless skin, her pale yellow hair, and inch-long black nubs that make it obvious that I'm way more human than demon…

Today, two of the three butterflies that came to keep me company hover over my head, shadowy wings sending my hair wafting in their slight breeze as usual. The third settles on the skirt of my dress, antenna twitching as though asking me how I am.

Been better, I muse, holding out my hand.

The butterfly leaps from my thigh to my outstretched finger. Its glow makes my pale skin gleam beneath its shadows.

I sigh.

I'm delaying the obvious. I know I am. It's only a matter of time before I'll have to confront my parents again. I'm not worried about Dad's reaction. He's always been happy to let Mom take the lead where I'm concerned, both as a kid and now as a grown half-demoness. And though I'm already a quarter of a century into my immortal life, she still treats me as though I'm a child.

Like the butterflies being my constant companions, Mom's overprotective side is just something that's always been. I'm used to it, and considering I was abducted as an infant, I understand it—but that doesn't mean I *like* it.

I'm a shadow traveler. I can't help that any more than my mom can help her desire to keep me coddled and safe. While not all demons in Sombra have a magical gift—unless, well, you're a mage—something about having one human parent and one demon parent has meant that me, Stevie, Rafe, and Clara all do.

Stevie takes after her human mother. With a voice like an angel, and a persuasive lilt to the sound that makes her a siren, she can talk you into anything with a few sung words.

Rafe was born with a mage's purple eyes, just like his demon dad. He's not the greatest when it comes to spells, though he can intuitively create a protective barrier made of shadows that protects anyone inside of it—and blocks anyone on the outside from breaking in.

Clara is younger than the rest of us. Barely a decade, we weren't sure if the daughter of the head of the duke's guard had a gift until she disappeared into her shadow form so completely, not even her mother could find her.

I wish I had *that* gift. I don't even have a true shadow form, not like the others with Sombra demon blood. They can go from their solid forms to their black shadows before fading away, leaving only a shimmer to indicate they're there. I can turn to mist sometimes, but that's just when I'm around people who don't believe in demons.

If you know I might be there, you'll see me. If you're sure I can't exist, I'm never there.

I think that's why my mist only works on my infrequent travels to my mother's home world, Earth. Duke Haures's first law says that the mortals from that plane aren't allowed to know about Sombra unless they, like Mom, are fated to belong to a Sombran. I've lived my whole life in this realm. I *am* a Sombran, and I know better than to let some human be the reason I'm sent away in chains to stay in the duke's dungeons.

But that's the problem. I don't have a shadow form, but my gift? I can make shadows work for me. I don't need to be a mage to create portals out of magic. As a shadow traveler, a shadow *walker*, I can move through the darkest patches and end up in a whole other world.

I've discovered three previously hidden neighboring realms over the last few years simply because I was curious, and, truthfully, because Rafe gets his kicks egging me on.

He did today, and we ended up lingering longer than I meant to in Brille Rouge. My mom spends most of her afternoons at the library with the clan mother. As long as I grab Rafe by his collar and drag him back to Sombra, I won't worry her too much with my excursions.

I'll worry her, of course, but not *too* much… unless I return home hours after we should've and, instead of facing my parents, I'm sitting on a lump of burnt wood a few homes down from where Rafe still lives with his parents.

His mother, Kennedy, is just as protective of Rafe, something that's only gotten worse since she realized that Loki *knocked her up* again.

Knocked her up… it's such an odd expression. Growing up in Nuit, I knew what the gold moon meant for bonded mates long before I had any understanding of what the act of mating was. Now, at a quarter of a century, I do, even if it's the mechanics only. Still, just because I'm a virgin waiting for my mate doesn't mean that Rafe and Stevie and I don't fantasize about the demons or demonesses who the gods have chosen for us. But *knocked up*? Loki didn't hit Kennedy. He *fucked* her, and if that's another word I've learned from my mother's native human language, I like the sound of it better than *mated*.

If it's up to *my* mom, I'll never *have* a mate—

"Alana? Alana. Ah. There you are."

Another sigh, and I brace myself before turning to look over at Mom. "How did you find me?" I ask, the words out before I can even think to hold them back. "Binx?"

She doesn't seem to mind. Her pretty face eases as the worry slips away. Moving purposely toward me, plopping down on the log beside me, she bumps my shoulder with hers. "I followed the butterflies."

That makes sense. Binx is too loyal. My pet ungez would lead Mom all around the village before he brought her to me when I obviously wanted to be alone.

But the butterflies? They don't know better, and now I have more company.

To outsiders, most might consider us sisters instead of a mother and her spawn. My father's essence has frozen my mother at the moment they finalized their mate bond. She's closer to sixty in human years, but looks to be the same age as I am.

When she gives me that knowing look of hers? She's pure *Mom*.

"I missed you today, baby," she says, and I don't even bother reminding her that I'm no longer a spawn. I'm Shannon's 'baby', and even after centuries have passed, I'm sure I always will be. "Where did you go?"

Shit. It's another human word, a curse from her old life that doesn't have a direct translation in Sombran, but it matches my feelings well.

I don't lie. Not to my best friends. Not to my parents. Not to the clan leader and his mate. Now, that doesn't mean I don't sometimes improve the truth a little, but if Mom asks me a question like that, I'll answer her even if I really, really don't want to.

Trying to tell her that I didn't use my special power to go exploring is useless. She knows.

She always knows.

With a casual shrug, I tell her, "Just for a walk."

A *shadow* walk.

Mom nods. "I thought so. You didn't go to Earth, though, did you? 'Cause I'm sure I mentioned that it might've changed since I lived there." Under her breath, she says softly, "Every time I go back, it does."

I give my hand a tiny shake, letting the butterfly take flight so that I can lay my fingers gently over my mother's.

Mom has always wanted me to have some idea of the world that half of me is from. That's why, over the years, she would go back with Dad and me, showing us around while we followed the duke's decrees and stayed hidden in the shadows. I used to enjoy those trips as a family, but the last time we went, Mom discovered that her parents no longer existed.

Humans don't live forever. Neither do demons since, one day, we might choose to end our endless existences on our own. But humans? They barely get a century, and my mother's parents didn't even have that before they were gone.

That hurt her, but she admitted to Dad that she always knew that was a possibility. Actually, what upset Mom almost as much was finding out that something she called The Beanery had disappeared as she was once again walking the same streets she'd left behind before I was born.

The Beanery… I don't know why a shop devoted to selling only legumes would've left such an impact on Mom, but there are sides to her that I'll never understand, even half-human as I am.

She mourns a world she's no longer a part of, even though she swears—and shows—that she's happy living in Sombra. And yet, as worried as she is that I'll run off to the human world alone, she slips her hand out from under mine, patting the top of my fingers, and says, "If you ever want to go there, just tell me. I'll go with you. Probably not back to Jericho… not like I think anyone from the old days will remember me…" She pauses thoughtfully. "It's been twenty-five years, but you know what? Mrs. Winslow is probably too nosy to die yet so, with my luck, she'd see me if I did go back again." Mom shakes her head, soft yellow, nearly white hair the same color as mine swaying with the motion. Behind her, a butterfly flutters at the same time, mesmerized by the sway. "Screw New York. Let's try Paris. Or London. You'd like that. With your powers, Alana, we can go anywhere."

That's another problem right there.

Not that Mom is trying in her heavy-handed way to appoint her and Dad—because wherever Mom goes, Dad will surely be right there, forever her shadow—as my chaperones. She is, and this isn't the first time, even if she insists that she doesn't mind my adventures with Rafe, but it's the idea that my gift makes it so that I can visit any and all worlds.

Until today, I thought that was possible.

And then, on Rafe's urging, I tried to open a shadow portal to a new world we heard about while we were in Brille Rouge. In between his flirting with one of the seamstresses he thinks he might convince to accept him as her fated mate, she told us all about how a cadre of soldiers from a nearby fire realm have been marching through their villages, searching for… something.

Katrin thought they were looking for mates. She wasn't sure, and with a shy smile sent toward the charming Rafe, she admits that the demonesses in Brille Rouge prefer Sombra demons if they can't find a partner among their own people.

Hearing that part of my confession about where I *did* go today, Mom's smile returns. "Everyone wants to belong to a Sombra demon."

She's a prime example. My parents have been mated for nearly three decades—almost as long as my human mother was alive before she summoned my demon father to her—and they couldn't be more in love.

I nod. "Katrin has her pretty pink eyes on Rafe, too, but as soon as she told him they were looking for something, he wanted to go check out their world. We've never heard of it, and… you know Rafe."

"You can't tell that boy no," Mom agrees. "Sometimes I wonder if he got some of Loki's feral side in him."

Honestly? I grew up with Rafe, and I wouldn't put it past him to be as wild as his father. Our village mage spent a century in the shadows, something I can respect, and while Rafe avoids them like he would the mate sickness, he's more like his father than he'll ever admit.

"So I tried. If only to get him to stop pushing me to do it, I tried to open a portal to Noctavara."

Okay. Like me, Mom is basically colorless.

Right now? She suddenly goes *white*.

"Alana. *Where* did you try to go?"

The strange note in her voice tells me that she doesn't mean my trip to Brille Rouge earlier.

"That's what's wrong," I admit, looking down at the ash beneath my boots. "I don't know. It was… closed."

Nothing's been closed to me.

I failed. I don't like to fail. Even after my nose started dripping dark blood and Rafe told me that it wasn't worth it to sate his curiosity, I pushed and *failed*.

That's why I slunk around the back of his house, dropping down on the burnt log and stewing over my failure as I dug a hole in the ash field with the tip of my boot. Because while Rafe gave up on spying on these unfamiliar fire demons, something told me that I *had* to get past the block.

I had to break through it.

I had to go to—

"The name. What did you call that place?"

Oh. Right. "Noctavara."

In Brille Rouge, their demon dialect—that they call Brilliant—is similar enough to Sombran that there is rarely any miscommunication between Katrin and her sisters and Rafe and me. We understand each other far better than if we went there, speaking in our mothers' human language. Noctavara might mean something else to Katrin, but that's what she called the realm.

Huh. Is that why I couldn't break through? Maybe… maybe that's not its true name—

"Don't go."

My head jerks, looking from the ash to my mom's face. She looks even paler, her dim blue eyes so different from my glowing gold ones. "Mom?"

"Don't go," she repeats, easing her hand away from mine. She swallows roughly, hiding the sudden concern behind a shaky smile. "Not until you're ready."

That doesn't make sense. Wasn't she listening? I told her I couldn't go. That it was blocked. She heard that, right?

Why doesn't she ever listen to me?

I open my mouth, but before I can say another word, she tucks a stray strand of hair behind her ear as she rises to her feet. "I have to go talk to Mal." *Dad.* "Dinner's in the fridge." The icebox that Rafe's dad spelled to keep our food cold in a mimicry of something Mom had back in the human world. "Don't stay out too long, sweetheart. Okay?"

She bends over quickly, pressing a kiss to the top of my head. The butterflies scattered as she lowered her face down to mine, but as Mom makes her excuses and basically bolts back in the direction of our home, they return to flutter in front of me.

My mouth is still open, the words stuck in my throat.

I swallow, then ask the butterflies, "What did *that* mean?"

But they don't know, and neither do I.

AUTHOR'S NOTE

Thank you for reading *Shannon in Sombra*!

While book eight might be the finale of the series, we're not quite done with these characters yet! Coming in August, the long-awaited prequel featuring Haures and Susanna will finally release.

After that?

Well, I couldn't tease Alana's future and her tie to Noctavara and just let it go, could I? Shannon and Malphas's daughter will have her own duet, with the first book coming out in 2026!

Keep scrolling/reading/clicking for more information about the two — and I hope you're reading for more Sombra demons in the future!

xoxo,

Sarah

For twelve years, this book has been my life— but I didn't know it was only just *starting*...

When I was sixteen years old, I found this old, leather-bound spell book at a garage sale. Something about it drew me to it, and when I noticed that it was written in an unfamiliar language, I decided that I wouldn't stop until I could read it.

I obsessed over it all through the rest of high school, then college. I couldn't get past the idea that it could be a *real* grimoire, telling myself that it would be super rad to be able to use magic, or maybe even travel to another world like in that movie from a couple of years ago, *Labyrinth*. After all, wouldn't it be great to find my very own Jareth?

For some reason, this book has always made me feel like it was the answer to my happily-ever-after. And when I translate the *Verus Amor* spell and discover it really is a true love spell, I decide to give it a try.

Instead of a Goblin King, though, I accidentally summon a fearsome horned man into my home. With colorless skin and glowing blue eyes, he crooks his claw imperiously, expecting me to follow him. And when I don't? He leaves before returning with a shadowy creature—and a pair of gold chains for me.

Next thing I know, I'm pulled to another world and thrown in a dungeon cell, Duke Haures's human prisoner. At least, that's what I think I am.

The powerful demon duke? He knows better.

He knows that I'm the one true mate he's waited millennia for… and he'll do anything to keep me.

But do I want to stay?

KEEP IN TOUCH

Stay tuned for what's coming up next! Follow me at any of these places—or sign up for my newsletter—for news, promotions, upcoming releases, and more!

SarahSpadeBooks.com
Sarah's Newsletter
Sarah's Signed Book Store

facebook.com/sarahspadebooks
x.com/stressie
instagram.com/sarahspadebooks
amazon.com/author/sarahspade

ALSO BY SARAH SPADE

Holiday Hunk

Halloween Boo

This Christmas

Auld Lang Mine

I'm With Cupid

Getting Lucky

When Sparks Fly

Holiday Hunk: the Complete Series

Claws and Fangs

Leave Janelle

Never His Mate

Always Her Mate

Forever Mates

Hint of Her Blood

Taste of His Skin

Stay With Me

Never Say Never: Gem & Ryker

Bound by the Moon

Sombra Demons

Drawn to the Demon Duke*

Mated to the Monster

Stolen by the Shadows

Santa Claws

Bonded to the Beast

Fated to the Phantom

Claimed by the Creature

Grabbed by the Guard

Taken by the Twins

Shannon in Sombra

Sombra Demons (next generation)

Tell Them That I'm Coming

Stolen Mates

The Alpha's Heart*

The Feral's Captive

Chase and the Chains

The Beta's Bride

Wolves of Winter Creek

Prey

Pack

Predator

Protector

Sanctuary

Watch Me Burn

Make Me Bleed

Murder in Moonburrow

Fake It 'Til You Mate It

Play Dead, Stay Dead

Beasts of Blackmoor

Trick or Beast

Christmas Eve with Krampus

Just Right

Big Bad Wolf

Claws Clause

(written as Jessica Lynch)

Mates **free*

Hungry Like a Wolf

Of Mistletoe and Mating

No Way

Season of the Witch

Rogue

Sunglasses at Night

Ain't No Angel

True Angel

Ghost of Jealousy

Night Angel

Broken Wings

Of Santa and Slaying

Lost Angel

Born to Run

Uptown Girl

A Pack of Lies

Here Kitty, Kitty

Ordinance 7304: the Bond Laws (Claws Clause Collection #1)

Living on a Prayer (Claws Clause Collection #2)

Diamonds are a Witch's Best Friend (Claws Clause Collection #3)

9 781961 594449